Jeffrey Lyman

Fantastic Tales of
Steampunk

PAPER
PHOENIX

PRESS

Pennsville, NJ

PUBLISHED BY
eSpec Books LLC
Danielle McPhail, Publisher
PO Box 242,
Pennsville, New Jersey 08070

ISBN: 978-1-956463-99-6
ISBN (eBook): 978-1-956463-98-9

Cover and Interior Design: Danielle McPhail, McP Digital Graphics

Art Credits -
Cover:
Steampunk ornate metal frame © TStudio, www.shutterstock.com

Section Break:
steampunk installation © jro-grafik, www.fotolia.com

Dedication

For my best friend, Danielle,
who always pushes me to work harder and aim higher.

CONTENTS

The Fall of Autumn

"Am I pushing them too hard?" Julia Destora asked, wiping Bracken blood from her leather apron with a towel. She tossed the towel over a rack near the steam boiler and warmed her chapped hands. Her dress was stained with smoke and sweat, and her light brown hair was pulled tightly into a braid. It was no way for a gentlewoman to appear before her patron, but Julia was a bridge builder first and foremost, as Lord Farelle knew.

"Five bridges are a lot for one day," Lord Farelle said, lifting Julia's hand to inspect the red, cracking skin along her knuckles. "But we need to be thorough. Do you want better mittens?"

Technicians in dusty coats hurried out into the warehouse carrying a new drive-box. Julia smiled.

"We've crossed to the same place five times in a row," she said. "I'll figure out the connection between wheel-speed and the angle of the drive-box, but for now at least we know we can return to places we've been. And my mittens are fine."

"I'm proud of you." He placed a hand on her shoulder, and she basked in his words. "Your speed governor will get us home."

"The governor is just one component." But she *would* get him home someday. All of them trapped in New Ange would go home. "For years I've played with belt lengths and materials," she laughed, "and it was wheel-speed all along."

"You couldn't have known."

"Somebody knew once, when they built the Great Bridges."

"And we'll relearn if it takes my whole life and fortune," he said. "I *will* see my family again."

"Then let's run the last test and close up shop."

"I'll direct the hydrogen guns as always. This has been a bad test sequence."

"Five gates, five Bracken attacks." She shook her head. "There's a connection there too."

They walked into Lord Farelle's warehouse, a bustling place of construction and destruction. Warm afternoon sunshine poured through windows overlooking the Anvil Bridgehead. The mighty span of Anvil rose in a soaring arch a dozen paces wide up from of the steep, clay banks of the River Alama, and stopped abruptly halfway across at a shimmering gate. Somewhere unreachably far away, its other half descended into the city of New Belany.

Anvil was one of just four Great Bridges left in New Ange, and Julia's heart yearned to rediscover how the ancestors had created such magnificence. Up and down the banks of the river lay the ruins of other bridges—lost pathways to lost cities. Rusted iron girders and carved rose-marble cladding thrust above flowing water everywhere.

But for now, Julia had a test to run. Her technicians adjusted steam flow to the pistons that drove her fifteen-foot flywheel sunk deep in the floor. Two reciprocating rocker-beams above swung back and forth, driving cranks as thick around as her waist. The rough, oak floorboards of the warehouse shook as the flywheel came up to speed.

"Ready?" Julia shouted above the racket.

"Open the gate!" Lord Farelle called down from the bank of riveted hydrogen tanks on a catwalk.

Julia glanced up. He was sweating, his face bright red in steam blow-off, but he grinned and his eyes gleamed fierce. To Lord Farelle's right and left, technicians gripped hydrogen nozzles. Pilot flames flickered at the ends of the barrels.

"Engaging." Julia checked her tight braid. Rule number one in building a test-bridge was to keep your hair out of rotating machine parts. Her scalp crawled. Rule number two was be ready if the gate opened and Bracken attacked. With today's mechanical speed setpoint, a Bracken attack was a certainty.

She eased a lever to nudge a gear, making contact with the flywheel's teeth. The flywheel turned at a paltry ten revolutions per minute, and Julia's engaged gear leapt to life at nearly two thousand. She'd calculated the gear-ratio and stamped the teeth into the brass herself.

Another technician squeezed oil over the marriage of gears and Julia breathed the soothing scent. No reason for nerves.

She pulled on leather gloves and tossed the end of a belt around a spinning axle. The belt stretched almost twenty feet to the newly installed drive-box above her sixth bridge.

The bridge was only a truss, with plank-decking in an arch that rose to the height of Julia's waist. She preferred rough construction. Some bridge-builders used iron and scrollwork in their designs, but she didn't have patience for such frippery. The five test-bridges she'd built today were cut in half, their drive-boxes vanished into the aether. Iron-work was wasteful.

"Engaging the tensioner!" she called, pulling back a second lever and forcing the axle against the spinning belt, taking up slack. "Get ready!"

She and her assistant hefted pneumatic flechette-rifles and trained them on the nascent gate atop the bridge as transmission gears inside the drive-box dropped into place. With a *whump* of air that pulled smoke and steam past Julia's head, the bridge's far side vanished. The belt connecting the flywheel to the drive-box was cut as a gate shimmered to life at the bridge's abrupt terminus.

Julia held up a glove as the end of the cut belt whipped through and over the axle, but kept her eyes focused. Any second now...

Flying shapes erupted from the gate with high-pitched yowling. The Bracken were filthy things about the size of a bulldog and covered in matted black hair. They seemed to be half mouth and half ass, held aloft by blurring wings.

"One, two, three…" Julia counted as bright gouts of burning hydrogen embraced the beasts and they spiraled up, shrieking. "Four, five…" There were never less than four in a flock, rarely more than eight. "Six, seven…" Technicians with buckets ran to douse burning Bracken where they dropped.

Two Bracken arced below the flames, loose in the warehouse. "Two free," Lord Farelle bellowed.

"I see," Julia whispered, and tracked the nearer one with her rifle, leading it in its bat-fluttery flight. *Pffpt*. The tank by her hip released one hundred and fifty pounds of air through its reinforced hose, and a flechette the size of her finger knocked the thing from the air. She reached for a second flechette.

Then she heard screaming. She swung around to see the second Bracken latch onto a technician, pulling him into the air. Her assistant stood frozen, horrified, his empty rifle at his shoulder. Other technicians scrambled toward the screaming man with an arm deep in the Bracken's mouth. Julia slid open the breach on her rifle and shoved the second flechette into place. Pumping the bellows hard with her boot to regain some pressure, she aimed and squeezed the trigger.

The moment the flechette flew she dropped the rifle and grabbed a coal-shovel, striding around the turning flywheel toward the tug-of-war between the beast and the men on the floor. The Bracken foundered; her flechette had lodged in its side, snagging its wing. Julia waited, grim. Blood streaked down the technician's arm from his mangled elbow.

After a few seconds the Bracken dipped low and Julia clubbed it with the shovel. She swung the shovel again, overhead like an axe, and the creature collapsed, shrieking. She chopped the blade into its brain then flung the tool away.

"Get him to Doctor Spraguss," she ordered as someone wrapped the man's arm in a towel. Then she turned on her assistant.

"I'm so sorry, miss," he stammered.

"You *must* stay alert when we open a bridge," Julia barked. "We all miss sometimes, but it's unacceptable to freeze. Where was your second flechette? Go! Help carry him to Doctor Spraguss." She glared as he ran past.

Lord Farelle joined her and nudged the bloody Bracken with his toe, his lip curled. Its remaining wing was folded down its side. It had vestigial legs, blind eyes, and almost no ears. "At least they burn well," he said.

"I am pushing the men too hard," Julia said, looking for another towel to wipe yet more blood from her apron. "I'll visit him at the doctor's," she said. She would support his family while he recovered.

"Julia!" bellowed a voice from the end of the warehouse.

"Perfect timing," she muttered, her stomach tightening.

Her father, Malcolm Destora, shoved past the technicians carrying the injured man. Malcolm was big, with heavy features, a lined face, and proud sideburns. He was a respected professor at New Ange University.

"Are you all right?" he demanded.

She blanked her expression. "I'm fine, Father." She didn't like him barging in on her work, seeing her so filthy.

Malcolm pulled up short as Lord Farelle's men roped one of the smoking Bracken and began dragging it toward the steam boilers. He gripped his walking cane like a club.

"Is something wrong, Father?"

"Wrong?" he sputtered as the Bracken corpse left a soot streak across the floor. "I came to invite my daughter to dinner and witnessed flaming beasts through the windows. Men are being carried out."

"The man will live," she said, keeping her tone civil.

"Julia!" her father snapped.

She turned to the windows, not wanting a fight. People crossed the Anvil Bridge in a steady stream.

"Julia," her father said again.

"We are fine," Lord Farelle interjected.

Malcolm whipped around to face him, his cane up. "With all due respect, Lord Farelle, this is a private conversation."

"Enough!" Julia said. "I will dine with you, Father. First I must finish and change into something suitable."

"Finish?"

"If you want to dine, you wait." She turned to Lord Farelle. "Where is my cold-weather gear?"

He snapped his fingers and a servant rushed forward with a fur-lined coat. Next came mittens, a scarf, and smoked-glass goggles.

"I'm coming with you!" her father insisted.

"Not in that, you're not." She threw off her apron for the sixth time that day and pulled on the coat. Her chapped hands protested the mittens. "It was sixty-two below this morning, and it's only warmed to forty-five below after the day's sun."

"See me when you get back," Lord Farelle said. "Good night, Malcolm."

"Lord Farelle," Malcolm said stiffly, then hurried to grab a coat.

"Would you please rethink this?" he said as he caught up to her. "How many times must you tempt the Bracken?"

She grabbed a rope as she strode to the test-bridge. "I like to watch them burn." She tied one end of the rope to an iron hoop in the floor and the other around her waist. "It's better than the alternative."

She refrained from rubbing the teeth-scars across her shoulder and back, a memento from when Bracken pulled her mother from her arms. That moment was often near her thoughts.

"You've built and broken more bridges than anyone since the ancestors. You are twenty-eight. Let someone else build bridges."

"If you want to get on with your life, that's fine," she said, a blunt comment on his new wife. "I am making progress."

He tied a rope around his waist, copying her. He'd never crossed a bridge into the wasteland before, and she wondered if he would think it beautiful.

"Don't let your zeal kill you like that Craggit fellow," he said.

Julia's eyes were drawn to a bridge at the end of the warehouse. What a waste.

They'd found John Craggit on the warehouse floor, his head eaten off and two Bracken buzzing about the room like angry flies. Without Craggit's notes there was nothing anyone could do with the bridge. It led to a trackless swamp, the only bridge to lead there, and Julia had crossed it many times.

"Mr. Craggit was reckless," she said. Her boots *thunked* on wooden planks as she walked up the bridge. "He was alone when he opened his bridge."

Her father joined her at the top where the gate wavered like steam. "Would you listen to me?" he said.

"Hush. Take a breath and hold it. When you have to breathe, inhale slowly or you'll freeze your lungs." She stepped through.

As always, the raw shock of the cold almost brought her to her knees. It was also blindingly bright, with a low afternoon sun skipping off countless ice shards. Her father followed her and gasped. Foolish, that. He'd better learn to breathe properly, or he'd suffer.

This half of her test-bridge was a color splotch on the vast plain of shattered ice-upthrust. Squinting, Julia searched for the jagged mountain that had become her anchor today. A few dozen yards away, five black Bracken marred the ice, already dead from frozen lungs. These were the ones who'd had the poor luck to burst through into this side.

Hah! There—miles across the plain. Julia had rotated around the mountain a fair distance this time, but she could still see both peaks. She pulled a charcoal stick and heavy piece of paper from her pocket and sketched them, trying to capture the bare, north-face and its angle; drawing in the broken dome of the nearer peak and its shoulder of snow.

It would have to be enough. Her shivers had grown so violent that she could no longer draw. She grabbed her father's sleeve, and he turned with her.

As always when she crossed the gate she looked up, hoping to see the missing drive-box at the moment of transition, but as always it was neither here nor there. Instead, the winter sky changed to clerestory windows and coal-dust dancing in sunshine. She inhaled deeply to thaw her throat and lungs, her nose too cold yet to smell oil, iron, or smoke.

"Did you get what you wanted," Malcolm demanded, clapping his hands together, his expression fierce. "Is that place worth your life?"

"I am learning, Father. Now let me bid Lord Farelle goodnight. We can eat at The Tarandess Club."

He didn't pursue her when she joined Lord Farelle next to his boiler. She still shivered terribly, and stretched her hands close to the boiler's firebox.

"I'll get you heavier mittens," Lord Farelle said.

She smiled. "Stop mothering me."

That night, Julia recorded observations in her journal. An oil lamp burned by her bed in the highest room of her father's house, illuminating walls of bookshelves packed with scientific instruments, journals, and mementoes from her lost home city. Her charcoal sketches from the wasteland were crude, but the drivebox angle on the bridge correlated to the angle she rotated around the mountain. She wrote her conclusion triumphantly. If she'd attempted one more bridge, she might have found the ruins of her first bridge.

She looked out her garret window, a bit giddy. She could see the Anvil Bridge and part of the Autumn Bridge farther along. A fair number of people still crossed—carters transporting goods; businessmen in carriages; late-night revelers. She longed to be one, but she had not set foot on a Great Bridge since she lost her mother. Terror struck her when she tried, and she *had* tried a number of times.

She looked down. The number 431 was carved into the bridgehead. All of the Great Bridges had numbers, though no one knew why. She hoped they correlated to RPM's.

Once there had been twenty-eight Great Bridges binding New Ange to twenty-eight sister cities in fertile lands. One by one the Bracken had attacked, severing ties. Somewhere out there lay

Julia's childhood city of New Pars. Somewhere lay Lord Farelle's New Rolle and his family. His sons and daughters would be in their thirties now.

Starting tomorrow she would learn the secrets of the drive-boxes. She might even learn the secret of the Bracken. Then soldiers could take the fight to the beasts.

God, how she loathed them.

She paged through her latest *Journal of the Society of Bridge-builders and Explorers* and stopped at the only surviving drawing of the ancients' drive-box. The much-studied engraving was a side view, with each component called out and labeled in tiny script. Brilliant minds had recreated it as the modern drive-box, but everyone knew there was something missing. Why else wouldn't it work? There was something just out of sight, lost forever with the engraving's top and front views. Something that made all the difference.

The accompanying article was by Lord Whichmar, a rival of her patron. His bridgebuilders were attempting bigger test bridges.

Julia snorted.

She flipped through the remainder of the journal. There were plates of an elegant flying ship suspended from a balloon, followed by a drawing of the same ship in flames. Most of Lady Appellain's balloon team had survived. No one had yet been able to cross the ring of mountains around New Ange to search for the lost cities that way, but Lady Appellain was determined. She was using oxygen to help her crews fly higher, because the passes between mountain peaks were very high indeed.

Julia scratched at the crescent bite scars that stretched across her left collarbone and across her shoulder blade. She and her parents had been running up the Turquoise Bridge, trying to get back to New Pars before the bridge fell. Julia had stumbled and her mother came back for her. Julia survived the bracken that bit her because of a surgeon quick with a pistol. She'd been twelve years old when she caused her mother's death.

A soft knock came at her door. Startled, Julia yanked her sleeve up. "Yes?"

"Julia?"

Her father rarely came up to her room, and he sounded uncertain. She pulled a wrap around her shoulders. "Come in."

He entered as softly as his knock, hatless but still wearing his coat, and took a seat in the chair near her desk. "I apologize," he said. His eyes roamed across her shelves. "I caused a scene."

"It's fine," she said.

"No, it's not. I have not been present in your life the way I should have, and I have not done right by you. I blame myself that you aren't out dining with friends or attending balls… or married."

He opened her book of collected drawings of New Pars. It had been popular among stranded and grieving refugees. "I should have introduced you to society, not left you to these relics."

"Relics are what I have *left* of home," she said, her lips tightening. "They're your relics too."

"There is no going back. New Pars is lost. New Rolle is lost, and all the rest. Build a life here, in New Ange!"

"Is that why you remarried?" she snapped, conscious of his new wife downstairs.

"I will love your mother forever," he said gruffly, a pained expression on his face, "but it has been sixteen years since she died."

"I remember it like yesterday." And she did. She still had nightmares.

"But why is returning to New Pars so important? What's there for you?"

"It's where I remember Mother, all right?! Other than standing on that damned bridge." She began to flip through the *Society Journal* while she regained her composure.

"Okay," he said at last. A wary look replaced the anger on his face. "May I help you build bridges?"

"What? No. Father, tell me what this is about."

He shrugged. "If I can't bring you into my world, perhaps I can join you in yours. Once a week? I'll bring lunch."

"You don't know the first thing about engineering."

"Teach me. It's been a long time since we were friends."

Julia guessed this concession came after he'd seen the technician mangled. "Very well," she said. "I'll teach you what I can, but no marriage talk."

He nodded and stood to leave. At the door he paused. "It was beautiful. The ice, I mean."

"I think so." She recalled that shattered vista with wonder.

Her father shivered instead. "What sins did our ancestors commit to be lost in ice and hunted by Bracken?"

Julia had no answer.

Julia worked at her bench on the warehouse mezzanine as light poured through the clerestory. She had been punching gears, but grew distracted by the activity below as technicians prepared to open a bridge. It wasn't her bridge. Daniel Ophinia, young and full of energy, experimented with alloys. Lord Farelle stood at his side, gesturing as he once had at Julia's side. He placed a hand on Daniel's shoulder and Julia felt the bitter sting of rejection.

Lord Farelle had lost enthusiasm for her speed-governor, and she couldn't blame him. They'd built and destroyed nearly two hundred bridges, and wasted the year. One bridge at a time, she had mapped tremendous ice expanses, from western mountains to ice-cliffs overlooking frigid seas. Lord Farelle was the one who had shared her passion, and she wished she could have made him proud.

She shuffled her notes, then wedged them between an oil can and a pair of calipers. She'd taken voluminous notes in the beginning. There had been many Bracken attacks, and she'd graphed them against the RPM's. Eventually her notes dwindled to the quantity of Bracken — and injuries.

Her father helped her as he had promised. To her surprise, Malcolm Destora turned out to be an astute student, stamping brass with a patient hand. Julia knew he had no interest in gears, so she let him escort her to society dinners. She appreciated his company. She grew to enjoy smaller gatherings and music.

She walked down the stairs to join the excitement on the floor. She did wish Daniel luck, though she was certain that alloys had no bearing on gates.

"Miss Destora," Daniel said joyfully. "Come down from your perch to help?"

Julia suppressed a frown. He was young, and no doubt saw her as a failure, an aging spinster among the dusty spiderwebs. "Mr. Ophinia. I pray you guide us in a new direction."

"I'll direct the hydrogen guns as always," Lord Farelle said. "Julia, would you mind taking your rifle?"

"I would be delighted," she replied dryly.

As Daniel and Lord Farelle coaxed the main flywheel into motion, she slid a flechette into the gun's pneumatic chamber. She placed a second and third in a row by her side.

The door of the warehouse banged open and one of Lord Farelle's errand boys burst through. "Autumn is falling!" he shouted. "Autumn is falling!"

"What?" Everyone froze. The cranks between the flywheel and beams rose and fell as steam rumbled. Julia felt a weight drop in her stomach. Autumn led to New Chiro.

"Calm down," Lord Farelle ordered the boy. He waved to his boilermen to divert the steam away from the wheel. "What's happened?"

"Autumn's shaking, my Lord, and Bracken have been sighted. The Lord Mayor's ordered out the sappers to knock it down. People are jamming the road, trying to cross."

"Damn it all," Daniel said.

Julia swallowed her fear as she remembered running across another bridge. "All right," she called, unclamping the pressure tube from her rifle. "We have a duty." She threw a portable tank onto her back. Her hands shook.

Like a storm breaking, the technicians burst into motion, grabbing rifles, tanks, and satchels of flechettes. Julia, Lord Farelle, and Daniel followed through the doors.

"I was too young to fight when the last bridge fell," Daniel said nervously.

"Have you defended a bridge, Julia?" Lord Farelle asked.

"Seven years ago, at the Cedar Bridge. I was a phosphor-sniper. The bridge before that was the Turquoise Bridge, and I was a refugee."

"When you lost your mother." Julia felt cold, but nodded as he continued. "I stood behind a flechette cannon that day and we weren't prepared. The sappers took too long to fell the bridge. It was terrible. We lost the forward cannons."

"How?" Daniel said.

"The gate failed, and Bracken came through thick as ink," Julia said.

Autumn came into view, and it was packed. Terrified people shoved through the gate in a slow-moving crush—families and merchants trying not to get trapped on the wrong side. The New Ange receiving grounds were choked with people. Soldiers with teams of horses dragged phosphor flame-throwers into place.

Julia recognized the cries, the tears, the stunned disbelief. How could anyone be surprised anymore?

New Ange sappers worked furiously at the bridge supports, pounding rivets from the iron trusses with pneumatic hammers. Over on the New Chiro side, their counterparts were surely working with equal determination.

"What do we do?" Daniel said.

"We find who's directing the defense," Lord Farelle said. He used his size to forge through the crowds, and Daniel and Julia followed.

At the bridge, a harried corporal took one look at them and waved them off. "We have enough rifles," he said. "I need people on the flechette cannons."

"Where," Lord Farelle responded immediately. The corporal pointed to the riverbank. Lord Farelle turned to Julia and Daniel. "Keep your heads down," he shouted over the crowd-noise. "They'll need you after the bridge falls. Rogue Bracken will be everywhere."

"We'll be ready," Daniel called back as Lord Farelle disappeared into the crowd.

Julia grabbed the corporal's sleeve. "Do you need anyone else at the cannons?"

He eyed her up and down. "How brave are you?"

"I'm a bridgebuilder."

He nodded. "Come with me."

Julia rubbed her back and crouched behind the iron shield riveted to the flechette cannon. Sweat plastered her braid to her neck. She couldn't believe she stood on a bridge with water rushing under her. All those times she'd tried to force her feet onto one, and this was how she finally managed it.

Fat pneumatic pipes wound from her cannon's sixteen rotating barrels to the bellows behind and to her right. The two haul-boys who had volunteered with her leaned tensely on pump-levers fixed to the bellows.

"Wait for my signal!" bellowed Corporal Kiret to the line, trying to be heard. "Let the snipers handle individual Bracken!"

Julia's crew was one of six cannons staggered in a V on the bridgehead in the thick of the throng. Ten more cannons had been dragged up and down the riverbank to sweep the bridge from the sides, their long cluster-barrels casting shadows on the river. Lord Farelle was there.

Lined up behind the cannon placements, six paces behind Julia, their bell-mouths wide enough to swallow a pumpkin, were the phosphor-flame throwers. Twenty throwers, massive double-bellows stacked behind with four haul-boys to each bellow, stretched in an arc that enveloped the cannons.

A buzzing thrum grew above the pounding of sappers' hammers. Julia's hands slid on the aiming yoke as sweat slicked her palms, and she wiped them on a kerchief. Breaks formed in the crowd, and late refugees were running. A man staggered through. Julia's breath caught as she saw two babies under his arms and a child clutching his back. His face was grim and determined as he lumbered down the arch past her. Bigger breaks, and she saw wounds on late runners. The Bracken were hitting the New Chiro side, but that could change like a shift in the wind.

Julia breathed, holding back panic. She wasn't twelve this time. She pressed her forehead against her shield, smelling thick, lubricating grease. Just breathe.

The buzzing drone deepened to a loud '*Brrrrrr*' and Julia lifted her head. "Here we go," she said, getting the same excited, sick feeling she got when she was opening a gate.

"Bracken!" someone shouted.

Flying black shapes burst from the gate as refugees ran below them. Julia cranked the elevator on her cannon to raise the barrels above people's heads. She prayed good luck for her friends and fellow bridgebuilders in New Chiro.

She heard the *pop-feeesh* of phosphor-sniper rifles, and the sky crisscrossed with white trails. Burning Bracken tumbled. Julia had been a sniper at Cedar Bridge, but that was nothing compared to flechette cannons in the teeth of the fight.

The Bracken grew thick. Rogue columns escaped into the blue sky like ascending flights of birds.

"Cannons!" shouted the corporal.

Pulse pounding, Julia pulled back her trigger-grips, opening air-stops, and released three hundred pounds of compressed air into the impellor and worm-drive. Her cannon's barrels spun to life with torque enough to raise the right legs off the ground and twist her with it. She used all her weight to pull the gun back down. Flechettes poured into the rotating chambers and sped from her barrels with the deafening ratchet of repeaters opening and closing. Her haul-boys pumped furiously. The air darkened with flechettes, and Bracken fell in droves. She grinned around clenched teeth.

Brave handlers charged onto the bridge, waving refugees down the ramp, trying to get them behind the flame throwers. Medics dragged the wounded, shooting Bracken off with flechette pistols at point-blank range as someone had done for Julia sixteen years ago. A woman staggered past, blood streaming from her hip.

Seconds ticked by at eight flechettes a tick, while the cannon rattled Julia's teeth. Sweat ran into her eyes. Runners rolled a new hogshead of flechettes onto her conveyer-carriage when she went dry—and the bridge swarmed. Black carcasses poured continuously into the Alma River.

She wiped away sweat. What the hell were the sappers doing? They were supposed to have worked out bridge-felling after the Turquoise Bridge bloodbath.

Then like a steam pipe rupturing, the swarm erupted into a roaring mass of black and teeth.

"Flame throwers!" cried the corporal over the howling.

Julia dropped into a hunch as Bracken dove down on her gun and the defenses behind her came to life with a *whump* that shook the ground. Blinding white streamers whipped into the Bracken flights above the cannons and Julia felt her hair singe in the purging fire. One—two—three seconds, the throwers fell silent with their fuel spent. Thick smoke draped the bridge and flaming Bracken rained down. In the silence that followed, Julia heard hammers pounding beneath her.

She squeezed her trigger-grips again, striving with the other cannons to turn aside the push by steel alone. Phosphor-loaders heaved fuel into the gullets of the flame throwers while their haul-boys pushed gauges to five hundred pounds per square inch. Another bridge-shaking *whump* and Julia ducked. The center throwers were firing straight over her position, hot enough to curl leather. The smoke stank.

She swung her sight to pick up a Bracken stream flying low down the bridge ramp, under the phosphor bursts. Her flechettes bounced and jumped off the deck. She would be overrun soon; she knew this and felt calm. The throwers *whumped* again, shattering the Bracken core.

"Get ready," Julia shouted to her haul-boys. Her hands jerked as her barrels spun. All she could see of the Bracken were teeth and throats, and her flechettes trailing into them.

Whump. Three, two, one.

She heard kettle drums. The sappers had finished and Autumn was falling, *Thank God!* She threw herself at the railings with the rest of the forward cannon crews.

At the rails, Julia felt, more than heard, the collapse of a main pier under the bridge. The side of Autumn dropped and Julia fell hard. Something struck her, rolling her. She felt tearing pain. She grappled with the Bracken chewing into her side, then tumbled blindly over the railing.

The beast tore free of her flesh when she hit the water. It tried to swim but she held it under, fingers dug deep in its fur. People fell all around her and she fought the thrashing Bracken until it went limp.

Looking up, Julia saw Autumn teetering, the iron of its remaining piers shrieking and bending. She was passing under it, caught in the river's current. Sappers dove clear.

The gate, still spewing Bracken by the hundreds, was distorting under the weight of so much metal and stone, its hazy borders writhing like snakes. Another pier gave way and Autumn twisted over. The flame-throwers fired one last time and Julia stared straight up into the gate.

She was able to see Autumn's massive drive-box for a bare instant, lit by phosphor-flames and burning Bracken. After so many centuries the great flywheel still turned, though it was horribly out of balance, rocking the assemblage. There was a second flywheel! What was that?

Then it tore itself apart as the bridge pulled it down. Autumn tumbled and the resultant wave threw Julia into the air. She could see the shoreline collapsing and cannons falling. People fought Bracken with axes among the flame throwers. The wave passed; the bridge was gone. White trails continued to cross the sky from phosphor-snipers, and would for days.

Julia drifted to shore, letting go of the dead Bracken. Her limbs were lead. When she tried to sit, she found that her dress and skin were shredded. She could see bloody rib bones. She felt light-headed and tugged fabric up as people raced toward her. Tired beyond measure, she lay back in the muddy water and closed her eyes.

"How could you volunteer for the cannons?" her father demanded, sitting by her hospital bed. Lord Farelle sat at his side. There were dark circles under their eyes.

There were many injured in the ward, more every day as the Bracken were hunted across the nooks and crannies of the city.

"I saw Autumn's drive-box," She replied triumphantly finally telling the news that had been bursting within her. She had so many stitches in her side that it hurt to breathe.

"Impossible!" Lord Farelle replied.

"I doubt there's ever been a bridgebuilder under a bridge when it fell, to see what I saw." She had relived that moment a thousand times over the past days of delirium and infection.

"And what did you see?" her father asked. Lord Farelle leaned forward.

She swallowed. "We're missing a flywheel, turned ninety degrees to the other."

"What's the purpose in that?" Lord Farelle said. "You proved the flywheel turns you about the ice."

"I know. But the vertical flywheel only rotates you around the vertical axis. There are two more axes."

"Wouldn't rotating around the horizontal take you deep into the ice? Or up into the air?"

"A flywheel along the x-axis would, but not the z-axis.

"And you think the fertile lands are on this… this other axis?"

"There's one way to find out."

Lord Farelle's expression turned ecstatic, but Julia's father cut through the moment. "Where do we even begin?"

She grinned. "With my speed governor and RPM's. Every Great Bridge had a number."

Lord Farelle stood, his eyes shining. "Julia, I trust you to recover quickly because we have work to do. I must prepare the warehouse. Thank you." He gave her a gentle smile before racing away.

Her father remained at her side. Once she and he couldn't have sat in each other's company, but working on the project had brought them closer.

She took his hand. "We could go home."

"I am home."

"You are as stubborn as I am," she said.

Julia nudged the small gear into contact with her great flywheel. It turned at 569 RPM, the number that once graced the Russet Bridge, Lord Farelle's bridge. He had been separated from his wife and children for twenty-six years and lost most of his fortune supporting bridgebuilders. His would be the first attempt.

One of Julia's assistants tightened the belt, and above the experimental bridge two flywheels, mounted at ninety degrees to each other, began to turn. It had taken her and her father months to figure out the linkage and mill the parts.

"Get ready," she shouted.

Dozens of men raised flechette-rifles. Other bridgebuilders, perhaps every bridgebuilder in the city, crowded close—friends and rivals, young and old. Patrons sat together in a raised box.

Transmission gears dropped into place and the two flywheels turned faster. Then the mechanism disappeared with a *whump* that sounded like music to Julia's ears.

Six Bracken flew from the newly forming gate, only to die in a hail of flechettes.

"See?" Julia said to her father as she pulled on her heavy coat. "They come through at the moment of instability. Are you ready?"

"I am ready."

She leaned on a cane as she climbed the bridge. Lord Farelle joined them, a phosphor-rifle at ready.

"Don't get your hopes up," she said to him. "This is our first real try."

He smiled, the skin crinkling around his eyes. "You can't stop hope."

They stepped through the gate into a hot, humid afternoon and a cultivated field. A boy waved and shouted.

"Is that a bridge?" he yelled excitedly. "Where you from?"

"New Ange," Julia said. "Where are we?"

"New Rolle," the boy said. "Oh wow. New Ange was gone forever."

Julia raised her face to the sun as Lord Farelle and her father laughed and threw off their coats. "Forever is a long time," she said.

The Troll King

Jack followed forty-seven other young men across the drawbridge and into the mighty castle of Klamp the Magnificent, the Troll King. It wasn't the scarred granite wall above, target of many catapult attacks, which slowed him. Or the heads on spikes, in a horrific row stretching to left to right across the battlements. Or even the massive ogres standing guard on either side of the gate. No, what slowed him were his twisted and uneven legs, which weren't cooperating today.

He'd already accepted his fate, and refused to let himself cry like some of the others. He was the eldest son in his family, after all, and at nearly eighteen, he knew he had to set an example for his brothers and sisters, and for his village. Next year it would be some other boy's turn on this drawbridge — some other eldest son.

Leaning on his stout hickory staff, making his feet move, Jack passed the two ogres all decked out in gray steel and leather straps. Jack stared enviously at the pistons and tracking gears at their knees. If he had something like that, he could walk behind the plow as well as his father. He could court one of the village girls.

Wishes were useless. Might as well wish he could fly as wish he had steam-driven legs like the ogres.

Jack passed from sunlight into the shadows of the entry tunnel, then back into the bright light of the castle's courtyard. Crowds clustered to watch the parade of eldest sons. Guards of all shapes and sizes stood everywhere: imps and ogres, trolls, even a fair number of men. They had tried to maintain a path for the boys to walk, but with the main crowd of sons already through and Jack lagging behind, the path had begun to break down. Grieving parents who had accompanied the boys moved toward the inner gate. Jack wished his family had come, but there was no money for travel, and they couldn't leave the farm untended for days on end.

Jack hurried, using his strong arms and his staff to push his legs more quickly. A few in the crowd jeered at him, no more than normal, but most were already focused on the spectacle inside. Some of their sons would survive, some always did, and the crowds loved to bet.

Beyond the inner gate, the crowds were shunted by a truly massive ogre toward the side stairs and the upper viewing galleries. Jack looked up warily at the fat, green beast towering over him. This one didn't even wear armor and rested a huge maul hammer on its shoulder. Jack barely came up to its belly-button.

He sped up again as a well-dressed young man in crimson velvet gestured impatiently from the door into the inner court. Jack was careful to keep his feet under him, planted as best they could, but he wanted to stop and touch that velvet. He'd never seen anything like it up close.

"You won't last five minutes," the young man smirked as Jack struggled by.

Jack held up for a moment, balanced carefully on his feet, and whipped his staff around into the back of the man's knees. As the man pitched forward, Jack smoothly continued the rotation of the other end of the stick across the man's ribs, then spun it around again and planted it before he toppled over.

"You didn't last *one* minute," Jack said to the man gasping and wheezing on the cold stone floor. He didn't think he'd broken anything. He'd learned the hard way how to handle the boys who wanted to cause trouble, after years of being shoved and tripped and punched. And once he'd started using his staff, he'd also learned not to hurt them so badly they couldn't work their fathers' farms. Life depended on the harvest, and you didn't do that to a family.

Just before Jack reached the inner door of the ballroom, the young man hurriedly limped past him with a glare. He couldn't retaliate with everyone watching, but Jack gripped his stick and touched the wall with his fingertips for balance just in case. He never took the shame of a beaten man for granted.

Emerging from the narrow entry hall like a cow into the slaughterhouse, Jack stopped, agape. He craned his head. He'd never imagined you could be in a space so large and still be inside. It was like standing in a vast field surrounded by towering trees, only the trees were stone and the sky was too. Great banners hung from every mighty column. The skins of the six kings the Troll King had defeated, along with those of their sons and their generals, were arrayed across the high walls. Stone ribs crisscrossed the ceiling in ornate patterns. Gas flames danced in braziers along every wall. The hall dwarfed the group of eldest sons and their guards. It dwarfed the crowded galleries of spectators. It dwarfed the six captive kings — younger sons or dissolute nephews of those who were originally defeated — on small thrones flanking the Troll King. It even dwarfed the Troll King himself, despite the mechanical armor that made him thrice as large as life.

Men made this? It had truly been a golden age of art and engineering before the Troll King arrived. There was even an ornate, raised pond built next to the king's throne.

"Eldest sons," boomed the Troll King from his throne of granite slabs, "approach. Be honored this summer solstice."

The guards had to push and shove to get the terrified group into motion. Even then the pace was so reluctant and broken that Jack had little problem keeping up. Feet shuffled across square flagstones as broad as a man was tall. He kept his head high as the swelling cheers and shouts and whistles from the galleries drowned out the other boys' whimpers. The galleries were alive with waving arms and smiling faces. Jack's attention was pulled from the vast room by the spectacle of drunk nobles thronging the upper galleries and commoners the lower. The whole six kingdoms must be here. He'd never seen clothing in such vibrant colors, all the colors of the six kingdoms in their loudest hues. One moment he felt naked in his linen tunic and trousers, and the next he wondered how you could move with so much fabric tangling your legs and arms.

The Troll King stood, and the galleries quieted. He was smaller than a grown man, misshapen, but he sat resplendent in the armor's seat with each of his limbs sheathed in leather and black iron, riveted brass and chains, gears and linkages. His legs extended three times as long as nature had gifted him, and where his feet lay visible in tight stirrups, massive, geared knees bent backward like a rooster's. Likewise, each of the long, mechanical toes of the armor's feet ended in sharp, curved talons. How could the six subjugate kings bear sitting next to him?

Jack, used to being far to the rear of crowds, found himself at the front as boys shoved back. He felt exposed.

"Now," the Troll King rumbled, "you are the finest young men of your small kingdoms." His gaze drifted across Jack, and he felt himself blush. "Or you are the ones lucky enough to get chosen by your councils. You will prove yourselves in three contests over the next three days. Those who survive will be granted six purses of gold, one from each kingdom. Enough to buy your home villages." He laughed to himself, a chuffing, grunting laugh. With a clanking clatter, his legs unfolded, and he rose higher than the armored trolls standing at his right and left. "The one I deem the winner will be granted an additional boon, if you amuse me."

His left arm, with a mechanical elbow near his natural hand just as the mechanical legs were knee-hinged at his feet, ended in a wooden cudgel embedded with iron spikes instead of a hand. His right arm ended in an armored mockery of a hand, each finger a knife blade. The knives clattered restlessly, and tiny puffs of steam continually erupted from the armor's joints.

Those nervous knives rose delicately and tapped a measure on the Troll King's armored chest. There was an occasional wet splash from the raised pond beside him as something breached the surface and then subsided again. The king leaned down and brushed the reflective water with the bare tips of his finger-knives, trailing ripples as everyone watched, mesmerized. Jack jumped along with everyone else as the king drove his knives down through the surface up to the wrist of the armor.

He swiveled back to his audience and raised his grotesquely elongated arm, lifting a large fish on the ends of the blades. Jack thought it looked like a carp, but it was mottled with brilliant golds and ivory whites. Then the king tugged his flesh-and-blood arm out of the armor and yanked the fish free. He bit deeply into its side.

"Even though they are my beloved pets," he said, chewing, "they exist for me to eat. Remember that." He tossed the remains of the fish onto the floor and shoved his arm back into the harness of the armor.

"I have had suits of armor made for you," he continued. "Three suits, one for each day of the challenge. Tomorrow you will be released into the King's Wood to be hunted by my hungry ogres, also in armor." Faces drained of color. No one wanted to face the ogres, their hunger was legendary. "Different challenges will greet you on the later days. Some of you will survive, many will not, so try to enjoy yourselves.

"Let the feast begin!"

Cheers from the galleries greeted his pronouncement.

The group of boys was quickly divided into six, one group for each kingdom, and seated at tables in a side room of a more modest size. The feast was greater than any of them had ever seen, though Jack knew that quite a few of his companions, as eldest sons of their villages, had some money. But village wealth was not city wealth, and meat was reserved for holy days in the villages. Jack dug into a great slab of pork with fervor.

He had hoped the six kings might appear to offer a benediction, and he wanted to see his king in Taurriggen blue up close. Instead, the boys endured a steady stream of lords and ladies and merchant princes sizing them up for the betting. The lords bore the same look on their faces as his uncle did when sizing up dogs at the dogfights. Who's fastest, strongest, hungriest? Some boys huddled over their food, heads down, others preened at the attention. Jack watched everything. A lady in flouncy Adhenion yellow could barely fit her skirts down the aisles between tables, while the lady in narrow-cut, Ghurian white behind her looked annoyed. An elegant, young woman in brilliant green with long, thick, chestnut hair stood by the far wall, her eyes far away.

One of the ogres clomped by in steam-armor, pounding the floor in wheezing, piston-driven steps, its bald head nearly touching the high ceiling. Flouncy yellow struggled to get out of the aisle while green's expression turned fierce and angry. She watched the ogre pass and then caught Jack looking at her. She turned and walked from the room at a controlled pace. Jack watched her go and then looked at the ogre. How fast could they run in that kit? They'd beaten the armies of men when the Troll King arrived from the west, but those knights had been running *at* the ogres, not away.

He jumped, startled, as someone tapped him brusquely on the shoulder. It was an older lord in a teal-checkered waistcoat with broad lapels and high collar. "Excuse me, boy."

"I'm Jack, son of…"

"Do you think you'll last more or less than five minutes?" The man held up a gold pocket watch on a chain. He smelled of sweet liquor. "I need to place my bet."

Jack glanced at the two bemused men standing behind and then back to the lord. "I plan on winning."

The man stood and barked a loud laugh.

"Oh," said Jack, faking a smile, "then by all means bet everything you have that I'll trip in less than a minute."

"Cheers." The man raised a pretend-glass and staggered off.

"Don't mind him," said one of the other two as they started to follow. "He gets excited during these games. It's all we've got."

The gas lights along the walls burned with a steady, sulfurous light so unlike the warm tallow candles of his mother's table. Jack watched the trio go, disliking everything about this cold stone place and the notion that these were just games.

The following morning, predawn, Jack was awakened from his pallet by a brightly dressed man banging a cookpot with a ladle. All the boys scrambled up from their rows of mats while Jack carefully levered himself to his feet with his staff. He'd slept with it, paranoid that one of the boys would steal it as a prank. Not that he'd slept much. No one had. Would dying hurt? Depended on how you died, he guessed. Hopefully it would be quick.

Upright, Jack saw that the summoning man was old, with white hair shorn close to his skull. He stood very straight and spoke in a loud, clear voice.

"You will be assigned a valet to assist you in donning your armor. Surprisingly, His Majesty Klamp the Magnificent, the First, has decided you will be outfitted with knives at your fingers just as our hunters are. What a blessing. I suggest you use the privy before putting the armor on, as it will be painful to do so after you are suited up. Come along."

As unluck would have it, Jack was assigned to the very man he'd knocked over the afternoon before. The grinning wretch, dressed in hunter-green velour, waved Jack into a changing room about as big as a horse stall.

"You are going to have so much fun today," he said. "You may call me William."

Leaning on his staff, Jack stared at William, suddenly afraid that he'd doomed himself by his show of strength the day before. He then looked over the heaped piles of rods, gears, leather, and metal before him. A fat, metal tank stood near the wall. "Let me guess," he said quietly. "You volunteered to dress me."

"It is my honor and privilege."

"I'm only wearing one arm piece, not both. I'm keeping a hand free."

The young man looked surprised. "The cripple is going to hold off the ogres one-handed? This gets better and better."

Jack sighed. "Are you an idiot? The ogres have arms like tree trunks. It doesn't matter if you have one set of knives or two when they hit you with a maul hammer. I need one hand free so I can hold my staff. I need it."

"Even in armor?"

"Get me dressed!"

The stirrups at the armor-knees turned out to be highly adjustable with metal plates and leather straps, in order to fit various leg lengths and foot sizes. Jack found that his twisted legs fit in snuggly and securely. It felt wonderful. His uneven legs and canted feet were suddenly perfectly aligned with each other. Maybe he wouldn't need his staff, though the thought of being without it frightened him.

"Can I stand?" he asked, trying to push himself up from his chair.

"Not until we connect the chest harness and the boiler. You need steam to operate the suit." William nodded to the riveted tank by the wall.

Jack's stomach sank. His chest and shoulders and arms were powerful after a life spent farming and maneuvering with his staff, but there was no way he could carry that thing. Especially while being chased through the woods.

William must have read his thoughts. "Don't worry, it's self-supporting once it's running. They want the ogres to kill you in a show of blood, not have you crushed under your own armor at the starting line."

"Get on with it."

William strapped the chest harness on and tightened it severely, then rolled the sloshing boiler tank into place and clamped it down.

"Got to get it heating," he said as he grabbed tongs. He picked up a heavy, black, iron box that radiated heat.

Jack leaned away from it. "What's that?"

"The firebox. It's packed with red-hot coals and chemicals. Should stay hot for a good long while."

"Where are you putting it?"

"Relax, you big baby. On your back with the tank. There's insulation so you won't feel it, and a smokestack to keep the smoke out of your eyes." William was sweating just holding the thing.

Jack leaned forward reluctantly as William bound the box in place with chains and hooks. It felt warm, but bearable. The stack extended about a foot up off of the tank.

"Now your arms."

"Arm."

"Of course," William sighed in a mock-irritated voice.

In minutes the arm was in place, twice as long as his natural arm, and too heavy to hold up for long. William set about connecting cloth-wrapped hoses from the suit to the boiler tank.

"You've done this before?" Jack said.

"Many times, though never for the solstice games. Armored combat is popular. People fight bears and tigers. Sometimes each other."

"Ogres?"

"Not ogres. The king wants the combat to last more than a few minutes of screaming. He reserves the ogres for political executions."

A short while later the tank started to bubble and rattle, and steam whistled wetly from the suit's joints. William had Jack stand up as he tightened various hoses and fittings until little steam escaped. Jack towered over him, and his smokestack nearly brushed the stone ceiling.

"Got to get these tight," William muttered. "Don't want you to run out of steam out there." He laughed. "What am I saying? You'll be dead long before your boiler goes dry."

"You're as comforting as my mother." But Jack was delighted. The suit did support the boiler and fire box, and suddenly his armored arm was easy to lift.

"Whoa," William shouted, ducking, as the arm swung wildly, finger-knives clacking. "Gently. Press on the levers gently."

Jack slowed down, gestured cautiously, and the arm responded. It wasn't graceful, it never would be, but it was functional and lethal, like a bladed club. His unadorned arm felt naked.

Gripping his staff for comfort, he took a cautious step. Then another, longer. He looked at William, grinning.

"Look at that," William said, frowning but looking like he was trying not to smile. "The cripple can walk. Maybe I shouldn't have put my money on you falling at the starting line."

"You shouldn't bet on death," Jack said.

"Death is all we have."

"Get me out of here. I can't breathe in this small room."

"Here's your helmet."

Jack looked down at the heavy-looking bucket in William's hands. "No. Won't do me any good against an ogre's maul hammer, and I want to be able to see and hear."

William tossed the bucket onto the table with a heavy *thunk*. "Duck when you're going through the door. I'll lose my bet if you bash your head *before* getting to the starting line."

Back in the immense hall, standing amidst forty-seven other boys bristling with uncomfortable and awkward armor, steam puffing, metal feet clomping and scraping on flagstones, the smell of axle grease and oil and smoke, everyone seemed swallowed by their armor rather than made larger by it. Armored ogres lined the walls from end to end, at least a hundred of them, grinning and joking back and forth in rough language. Jack pushed his hair from his eyes, conscious that he was the only one with a bare head and free arm.

Up above, the galleries were full. Wine and beer flowed. The next three days would be a celebration of the solstice games and betting and eating — the running of the eldest sons was just the start of it all.

A cracking boom sounded to his right, and Jack whipped his head around. More cracking booms. The ogres had started jumping, bouncing on their mechanical, back-bent rooster legs, rising higher and higher, crashing down on pistons and springs, lower and lower until they leapt back up again, higher than the boys' heads. They laughed raucously; finger-knives splayed and maul hammers thumping the stone floor.

"We're gonna die," the boy next to Jack groaned just as Jack was thinking, *Can I do that?* Jack noticed that the other boy had turned his whole body to watch the ogres through his helmet's eye slit. All the boys had clumsily turned.

"Get your helmet off," he said. "You'll see better."

"Shut up," the boy snapped. "You're gonna die first."

So Jack jumped, mostly to prove the other boy wrong. Gently at first, until he got the knack, then higher and higher. His mechanical legs absorbed the impact wonderfully, supporting his natural legs. He turned from the gaping boy mid-jump, crashing hard and leaping again, facing the ogres. Infuriating them. A number slowed their leaping as he continued, gripping their maul hammers in a less jovial stance than a moment before. Jack didn't stop jumping until trumpets announced the arrival of the Troll King.

The Troll King entered, followed by his six subjugate kings who tried to appear regal with their voluminous robes and retainers in matching colors. The Troll King was in a good mood as Jack settled down and backed up into the group of boys.

"To the starting line," the Troll King bellowed, gesturing with a great, clawed hand.

Outside, the sun had nearly risen, painting the sky a pale blue-gray. The troupe of boys was led to the side gate of the castle, the one closest to the King's Woods. Many boys struggled with their mechanical legs, stumbling over each rut and gully, but Jack found that he moved fairly well. A lifetime of staring at the ground had given him eagle eyes for safe paths. He quite enjoyed the walk, and being outdoors again where the sky was a proper sky and not a canopy of stone.

The six kings and their retinues accompanied the boys on the backs of magnificent horses in livery the color of their kingdoms. It was their job to represent the eldest sons of their small realms, and Jack's group clomped along next to the sky-blue of the Taurriggen Realm. Jack wondered if the kings ever used these games to get rid of the eldest sons of their rivals, or if it was always villagers' sons. He eyed his king out of the corner of his eye, not sure if he was allowed to stare straight at the middle-aged man with the short beard. The man looked kind, but Jack knew almost nothing about him. The Troll King was the one who set the laws, and his ogres enforced them.

The Troll King greeted them from atop the battlements over the gate in even beastlier armor than the day before. Great spikes extended up and down his armor's back, and Jack wondered how he sat down.

"Beyond this gate," he bellowed, "between you and the King's Woods, lies the parade grounds. Run for the trees. Scurry like rats. The ogres will count to one hundred before chasing but remember that ogres are not very good at counting past ten. Now off with you." The gates were drawn wide by horse-teams. A cheer arose from the massed crowd.

Jack didn't move as the near-panicking boys surged forward. It was old habit, letting the others go first, and he was glad of the reflex now as boys fell in the bottleneck of the gate, legs tangling. There were screams, and the sound of metal smashing against metal. Beyond, the first boys loped at league-eating paces toward the woods. Jack waded in behind, using his naked arm and staff to pry bodies apart.

"Get up," he yelled, seeking his own free path through and over the wreckage. "Get up! Go!" A boy below him was trapped in his armor like a turtle in its shell, steam venting freely from a torn hose. Jack leaned down and slashed through straps imprisoning the boy's arm with his finger-knives. "Get out. Run!"

He didn't have time to do more, as the counting ogres got tangled up around fifteen and sixteen and started skipping numbers. The downed boy yanked at buckles with his freed hand. Jack shoved through the gate and instantly lost himself in the indescribable joy of running. For the first time in his life, his legs were even and straight and strong. The backward rooster-knees flexed and bounced, and the bronze feet clawed hunks of dirt up behind him.

Arms pumped. Steam hissed. The contents of the tank on his back boiled. He began to pass clumsier, slower boys, weaving through them. The morning sun rose over the castle behind him, throwing his massive shadow forward onto the grass. He bounded.

Bursting into the woods below raised platforms crowded with the more avid of the noble spectators, Jack took note of the shouting. The carriage-path through the trees was lined with men and women—cheering, yelling, and drinking. Jack ran between them, feeling like prey being driven down a prechosen path. He'd been a beater often enough in his life, driving deer to the slaughter, that it was not a fate he wanted.

He veered left, crashing through the line of spectators and into the dim and dappled woods. Branches slashed at his unprotected face. He slowed to a walk to carefully lift and place his feet while a few drunken men followed him, laughing and cheering. They left him soon enough and he pressed on in silence.

He could hear the distant clank of metal runners and grunting roars of pursuing ogres. Jack circled back around to the start, beneath the nobles on the platform, behind the ogres. He was confident they wouldn't hear him coming over the frenzied roar of the crowd as he passed.

Reaching the hindmost lumbering ogre, Jack jammed his staff between its back and the firebox. It turned with a snarl, breaking buckles, and the firebox spun away in flaming sparks. Jack danced back and the thing scrambled after him. It didn't seem to have slowed any as it swung its gnarled maul hammer once, twice. Jack had just decided to chance turning and running when it staggered to a stop, panting. It took another step, laboring, and Jack knew its armor was deadweight.

He turned to the crowd and spun his staff with a flourish. "Have you ever wanted to kill an ogre?" he called, then pounded down the path away from the sounds of hooting laughter and the ogre's roar.

He now knew that knocking off the firebox wasn't going to do it. They'd get several steps and several swings in before their suits brought them down. He needed their suits to fail faster.

He skirted the armored corpses of boys in the pine needles, crushed and smashed into bloody messes where the ogres had vented their ferocity. He ran faster, more comfortable on the rutted path. Around a turn, a lone ogre brought his maul hammer down over and over on a dead boy. Jack ran past, snatching at the cloth-bound hose on the thing's back. The hose separated, hissing steam that blistered Jack's hand. He slowed and turned. The ogre looked at him confused, then dropped, its legs folding up on the knee. It mewled in confusion as its iron-clad arms slumped down. Then a cheering mob of drunk people rounded the curve in the trail, following Jack, lusting for ogre blood. Jack waved them at the beast and kept moving.

The hose was the weak-point, high on the boiler where only someone else in tall armor could reach. And with that realization, Jack sped up. More bodies but spaced farther apart. Jack hoped he could save some. As he ran his heavy feet thumped quietly down the path coated in pine needles.

He arrived at a clump of ogres soon after, clustered at the edge of the path on the lip of a ravine. Something had their attention, and they shuffled back and forth at the edge like they were trying to get down with too-big feet. Their squashed and piggish faces contorted and grimaced in concentration. Scar marks in the dirt indicated where someone had gone over.

In just two strides Jack passed them, yanking all five hoses as he went by. Steam vented wildly in his wake. The ogres tried to turn even as their knees folded. Two toppled backward over the edge. The trapped ogres snarled at him, scrabbling at the buckles that held them in their armor. Outside of their reach, Jack stepped carefully to the lip and looked down.

The boy who had initially tumbled down and started all of this was halfway out of his suit, still trying to free his legs. He had thick, dark hair and dusky skin—a son from the Kingdom of Triath. One of the more popular boys in the crowd this morning.

"You all right?" Jack called down.

"I'm okay," the boy shouted. Blood shone bright crimson on his temple where he must have whacked his head on the way down.

"Keep to the woods until sundown," Jack called back. "I'm continuing on."

"Thank you. I'm Peter."

"Jack."

"See you back at the castle, Jack," Peter said, and they nodded to each other.

And so it went through the day. There were few boys or ogres left in the open, just solitary figures hiding or hunting, so Jack tried to keep from sight. Five times he faced the beasts, jumping and dodging until he could get an opening. The reach of their maul hammers was terrible, but Jack's staff reached just a little bit farther.

Evening brought thirty-five of the original forty-eight boys back to the immense hall. They were filthy and exhausted, half-starved and thirsty. And Jack was a hero. Peter's telling of Jack's surprise attack on five ogres at once over the ravine grew with each telling. The galleries were far more crowded than they'd been the night before.

The Troll King raised one great knife-hand and beckoned Jack closer to the throne. Jack limped forward, balancing carefully. Falling on his face before the king was not how he wanted to end his triumphant day.

"A dozen ogres are dead," the king said flatly. Ogres muttered angrily along the walls of the hall. "That's more than any knight accounted for during the war. You caused terrible upset among the betting pools." The king glanced up at the upper walls of the hall where the gristly skins hung. "Should I mount your skin up there to appease them?"

Jack felt a chill run down his spine. "There's still two days left, Your Majesty. I'm sure your ogres will kill me tomorrow. Those who lay wagers can recoup their losses then."

"You're enjoying this."

Jack fought a grin. "I've never run so fast or so far, Your Majesty. Thank you for lending me the armor."

The Troll King glared at him a moment while Jack listened to the rustle of cloth in the galleries above. There was energy there among the people, though no one spoke. Finally, the king chuckled. "You'll not use that stick of yours tomorrow, boy."

Jack bowed. "Yes, Your Majesty." Whatever the contest, he just had to outrun the ogres. He'd proved he could do that today.

After a sumptuous feast and dramatic attention from lords and ladies—he had never spoken to so many women in his life—he lay on his thin pallet, exhausted and awake, staring at the ceiling. It seemed there were a lot more nobles coming and going at this celebration. He had seen the woman in green again briefly, looking at him, but then she disappeared. He didn't know why she intrigued him. She had character in her face and intensity in her eyes—like her thoughts were racing. He listened to the other boys breathing, calming his heartbeat.

What would tomorrow bring? Would it hurt?

After a light breakfast the following morning, Jack returned to his little stall to be outfitted. He recognized the boiler tank and hot firebox this time, but the piled contraption of cloth and metal bars and hinges was beyond him.

"You cost me a lot of money," William grumped happily as he burst into the room and swung the door shut.

"I'll try to remember to get my head stove in next time so you can collect."

"Nah, nah. I shouldn't have bet on death, right?"

"What odds are they giving me today?"

William shrugged. "The king's out for you now, so the betting is three to one you'll die on the starting line, five to one you'll make it to noon, and twenty to one you'll finish the day."

"Great." Jack pointed down. "What's that?"

"Wings. Today you fly."

"What?" Jack was horrified. Fly? With ogres?

"The wings'll do the work for you. Let them go and they'll flap and take you up. Pull them in a little and you level out. Pull them in more and you come back down. Simple, right? Lean left or right to turn, lean forward to go forward. You can't go backward."

"Simple, yeah. Except for the part about being in the air."

"And that everyone's wing-scaffolding is knife-tipped. The canvas of the sails is under a lot of stress holding you up. Anyone hits you with a blade and the canvas is going to shred. Down you go. The ogres have bigger wings for their weight, and longer knives. They'll hit you before you hit them if you go head-to-head. And don't forget their foot-claws."

"How do you even get close to them?"

William stared at him like he was an idiot. "You don't; you fly away. Don't stay in close and try to outmaneuver them either. They're clumsy, but they've got experience in the air. There was nothing we could do about them when the Troll King invaded."

Jack leaned back against the wall, taking some weight off his feet. "Your family?" he said gently.

William's face closed up, tight and strained. He nodded. "My father was Chief Steward to King Randolph."

"So why doesn't anyone fight? Use the armor?"

William gestured angrily back toward the hall. "Any armor we create is only half as good as this dwarf-made armor you're wearing. His Majesty gave you the good stuff because he wanted to show us all that we're no match for his ogres, even in quality armor. I think he likes to lose a few ogres because that keeps their anger focused on us."

"So let's show him something different."

"We plan to." William narrowed his eyes and dropped his voice to a whisper. "Forget about the betting and the odds. Survive. Live through the day, whatever it takes. We need you. The king executes two or three people a week for imagined crimes, high and lowborn both, so we've never been able to organize. People are terrified. But you showed them yesterday that it *can* be done."

"I was just trying to live."

"You fought back. We'll talk more tonight."

"So you're betting on me to survive this time?"

"I'd place my bet on life."

A short while later the first sons lined up on the battlements behind the rotten heads on spikes. The ogres today were quieter, more focused. Many stared at Jack.

The Troll King strutted by in gilded, ornate armor. He was very close, and Jack could see small horns twisting up through his hair. Jack's hand itched for a bow and arrows. There was plenty of unprotected flesh exposed by the armor, but the Troll King was rumored to be unkillable.

"There will be no count today," the king called. "The ogres will fly as soon as the first boy crosses the middle of the parade grounds. I would aim for the woods, if I were you. A tree might break your fall."

Jack looked down the line of eldest sons. They were bunched up and panicky. They'd be flying into each other on take-off, cutting wings. Jack decided maybe he should wait until the initial flight had cleared the battlements and risk the ogres. He stood a better chance against those lumbering beasts than against the crowd. He saw Peter looking back at him, and they nodded to each other. Peter's head had been bandaged after his fall into the ravine yesterday, and his eyes were blackened, but he had an intense look on his face. He was a survivor too.

"Go!" shouted the Troll King.

Boys immediately slapped release levers and wings flared out. Steam boiled. Wings swept down, cupping air. Cries and shouts. People were hit. Blood sprayed. Bodies rose in ponderous downstrokes of wings; bodies fell to the pavers of the battlements, wings in tatters. Jack waited, one... two... three, slapped his release lever, felt his wings spread and thrust down. His feet lifted. He arched back, leaning into the boiler despite the heat, turning over the courtyard, clearing the struggling boys with kicking feet and knife-tipped wings. He straightened, rising in shuddering hops. Higher. It was useless to try for the forest now, the front boys were already halfway across the parade grounds. The road before the gate was littered with bodies. Several boys hop-ran across the parade grounds, unable to take flight with holes in their wings. If they made the trees, it'd be a miracle. Jack concentrated on rising.

The castle complex, sprawled town, and forest stretched below him. The king's lake, vast and deep, lay on the other side of the castle. Still he rose. It was peaceful here. As he'd hoped, no ogres chased him. They could see plenty of boys right in front of them, and their hunter instincts focused on that.

He reached to his chest and closed the steam valve to the wings. They extended to their full width and stayed there, locked. Silence fell except for the bubbling boiler and distant screaming. Jack leaned forward and soared. Instinctively, he twisted left and began a great, banking spiral, just like the turkey vultures he watched on hot summer days. He could stay up here forever, except for the boys dying below. They needed him.

The ogres had corralled about half of the boys on the grass, circling, keeping anyone from running. Boys struggled to escape their deadly, tightly wrapped wings. Three ogres landed at a trotting run, maul hammers in hand.

Jack reopened the steam valve, pulled in his suddenly flapping wings, and dove. He had no foot-claws like the ogres, but he knew they were blind to anything approaching from above.

They circled low, moving left; Jack flared out his wings again, wingtip knives splayed, and banked into a right-hand spiral just above them. He came at them fast as they looked down at the spectacle below, and he slashed across the backs of four of them with blade tips. Metal raked metal as blades crossed wing-ribs, and he pulled up, flapping hard to gain altitude. Ogres followed him now, at least a dozen rising out of their circling. The four he had struck fell tumbling.

Jack remembered William telling him the ogres' suits were faster, but he was appalled at how quickly they rose. He needed to give the boys on the ground time. He needed to give himself time to reach the woods. Once he went into his dive, he'd be as blind as the ogres he'd knocked from the sky.

Two hundred feet above the grass, the lead ogres just three man-lengths below him, he hauled in his wings tight and dropped through them like a hawk in dive. Blind to everything but the approaching ground, he let the wings out a little, then a little more, sweeping, hurtling toward the woods. Trees below him moved by impossibly fast. He flared out his wings, hearing metal groan, and leveled out, smashing through treetops. He arched his back, swooping back skyward as three ogres smashed through below. Grunting roars—the pack was nearly upon him.

Using his strong arms and stomach muscles, Jack twisted and folded up, doubling over, yanking his right wing after him as he pivoted on his left wing. Again he dropped headfirst, but with his left wing still out he fell in a fast, nauseating spiral, like a spinning maple seed. Ogres passed him right and left, unable to pull up in time but still trying to slash him with their knives. His face hit cool, green leaves and he tried to stop his fall. The wings caught at everything, knocking him back and forth, wrenching his arms, while twigs slashed his face. He twisted and bounced.

Coming to a rest, body bent over, firebox upside down and sizzling, he heard the angry howling of the ogres above as they sought him. Hopefully the boys on the parade grounds had made it to the cover of the woods.

Jack looked back over his shoulder. He was still twenty feet above the forest floor, with no good way to get down, but he was alive. Cicadas whined and chanted. He began to release buckles to drop the boiler. He'd have to use belts, bands, and ropes to get down, and he wanted to get away from this spot quickly before the ogres landed and came looking for him.

He was alive!

That evening, twenty-seven of the thirty-five triumphantly limped into the ballroom. There were broken arms and legs, but never before had so many survived for two days. Jack walked with his old staff in the heart of the pack, a hero, Peter close by his side. He'd never been a hero before and was amazed at how his legs suddenly didn't matter.

The celebratory mood quieted at the sight of the grim Troll King. Everyone knew that the third day of the solstice games would be worse than the first two, but it suddenly sank in. Some boys started to separate from Jack, until Peter caught Jack's eye and nodded. Other boys, their spirits rallying, formed ranks around him.

Was it Jack's imagination, or were the six subjugated kings leaning forward on their thrones, eyes bright? Were the nobles of the galleries wearing more subdued colors, rougher colors, colors closer to the old battle standards of the six kingdoms? Was there an edge to the cheering? Were there more ogres along the walls? Was the Troll King himself wearing heavier, scarred armor? Functional armor? Jack had spent his life observing and knew things had shifted in the castle while he and the others were out trying not to die. He needed to speak to William.

The Troll King rose in a wheeze of steam, gears glistening with fresh oil. The legs of this armor were more slender, Jack saw, probably lighter and faster. The maul hammer on the king's left arm was chipped and cracked, as scarred as the armor. The right arm ended in a single, bronze spike instead of clattering knives. As one, the ogres took a step out from the wall, metal feet cracking and echoing on flagstones. With another crack they settled back on geared haunches. Spears came up. Something *had* changed in the castle.

"Did you have fun today?" the Troll King said to Jack in a voice like winter granite.

"Yes, Your Majesty," Jack said, bowing. "I never dreamed I could fly. Thank you."

"Will you enjoy it tomorrow, I wonder?"

Jack bowed again, unsure of how to answer.

The feast that followed was less playful than the previous two. There were more ogres and fewer betting lords. Jack ate ravenously with one hand, resting his wrenched shoulder.

Suddenly William dropped into the chair opposite and stuck out his hand. Jack shook with a firm grip.

"Thanks for winning me money," William said. "But you're not going to stay alive if you keep circling back to rescue people."

Jack shrugged. "Should I have just left them to die?"

"Are you brave, or crazy?" William said, his voice dropping.

"Does it matter?"

"They're afraid of you," William said.

Jack looked around the room at drunk nobles still laying wagers. "Who, the ladies?"

"Them too. They can't be associated with you right now, could be dangerous for their families." He glanced at the guards. "I mean the *ogres*. I've never seen anything like it." His voice was intense and excited.

"The ogres aren't afraid of me; they're not afraid of anything. They're waiting to kill us all tomorrow."

William leaned forward. "Maybe not."

"Why?" Jack said, then started eating again. "And don't be so obvious. I'm sure the king has eyes and ears."

William smiled and sat back, still speaking low. "The Troll King had forty-eight suits of armor made up for you combatants. Thirty-five made it back to the castle in one piece this year. I hear almost thirty of them went missing today while attention was on the games."

Jack shook his head as he laid his spoon by his bowl. "Now who's crazy?"

"I told you; you showed us it could be done."

"Thirty suits against hundreds of ogres? How's that going to go? And after? What do you think the Troll King will do to our families? And the towns and villages?"

William looked down at the table. "This is our first chance."

"Look," Jack said, "it's not that it's not a good idea to try something, but I don't see how it'll work. They say the Troll King can't be killed with mortal weapons."

William leaned forward. "What about you? You saw his face in there. You think he's going to let you live tomorrow?"

"I'll keep my wits about me."

"And you'll circle back around to help the others again, won't you?"

"Likely."

"There must be something..."

The young lady in brilliant emerald suddenly swept up and whispered in William's ear. Jack's heart sped up and he knew he was staring. She looked right back at him with an intense expression, then whisked away.

"Who was that?" Jack said softly, watching her recede. Her chestnut hair swept back and forth as she strode across the room. She was more beautiful, and fiercer, than he'd imagined.

William stood, smiling. "Lady Castiline of House Berou, and you'll never meet a more dangerous or brilliant woman. She's more warrior than all of us combined, and she just scolded me for speaking to you for so long." He stuck out his hand again. "Congratulations," he said loudly. "Be ready to dress bright and early."

"Making a show of it?" Jack said softly and shook the outstretched hand.

"It's all for show, didn't you know? Everything. Except when it isn't."

As William walked off in the opposite direction of Lady Castiline, Jack glanced around the room at the elegant, wealthy ladies moving among the boys — gently touching bandages and dramatically wincing at broken bones.

A show. Underneath it all, everything was deadly serious. And William wanted to use Jack to spark a revolution. Jack's heart drummed against his ribs, though he made himself chew slowly.

He'd run like a deer and flown like a hawk. He'd faced death in the ogres and won. He'd seen the bodies of nearly twenty boys sent home to their parents in wooden boxes. He couldn't return home and just tend goats and sheep as he used to, waiting for the darkness of night so he could swim without shame in the local pond. But he couldn't join a revolution either, could he? He was no warrior.

He turned back to the food that had lost all taste. He still had to survive the third day, and he didn't think he could. Nausea twisted in his gut, and he tossed down his fork.

The next morning, Jack once again couldn't recognize the armor. He saw a tank, taller and narrower than the usual boiler, but didn't see a fire box or a smokestack. There was a great, brass helmet with round windows of glass set into the front, sides, and crown. He tried to lift it and could barely heft it off the table. There was no way he could wear that. The rest... there wasn't much else. A few tubes, a few struts, and braces.

"What's it do?" he said when William came in. "Where are the knives?" Then he noticed that William was pale. "This is the end, then?"

William nodded. "It's a diving suit. A helmet and a tank of air, and not much else. There's a lever to pump more air into the tank when the gauge gets low, but you have to surface for that."

"No weapons? How am I gonna fight the ogres?"

William shook his head, his face pinched and tight. "The ogres are too afraid of the Kraken in the King's Lake. Won't go in the water."

"Kraken?"

"Big thing. About as big as three hay wains end to end. Lots of arms. It's fast."

Jack fell silent, thinking. "Can it come up into the shallows?"

"I don't think so, but the ogres will be standing along the banks. They want you in the deeper water."

"How does the thing hunt?"

"By sight. It has great big eyes. And splashing draws it. King Randolph's Sixth Regiment was driven into the water at the last battle. A lot of good knights. They say the Kraken grew ten times its size that day from the feast."

Jack stuck out his hand. "Thank you for your help the last two days."

William gripped his hand back. "We've got the armor," he said intently. "Maybe we can attack the ogres from behind before the Kraken gets you. I'll talk to Lady Castiline."

Jack smiled. "What, and waste such wonderful armor? Wait for a better opportunity. You'll only get one chance, so don't throw it away by attacking too soon, out in the open. If you do, the whole ogre army will come down on you."

"But you're going to die!"

"I'm not dead yet, so stop mourning. Now help me carry all this. Without the mechanical legs, I'm not steady."

The day was as bright and cheerfully sunny as the previous two, and the sun shone on clear, calm, black water. The Troll King had brought enough ogres to encircle the whole lake. About two hundred spectators clumped together between the castle and the water. Jack sat on the warm grass at the water's edge where William had placed him, surrounded by the other boys and piles of helmets and tanks. Everyone kept quiet.

"Face the beast of the depths," called the Troll King from atop his scarred armor, "or face my ogres."

The ogres spread around the lake stomped their metal feet on the grass. There were cheers from a few spectators, but the crowd had become muted. Out on the placid water, a few bubbles rose and burst on the surface. Jack felt ill.

"What do we do?" Peter said quietly. The other boys gathered around close, as if Jack had a magical answer that might save them.

Jack pulled the air-tank harness over his shoulders and turned his body so his feet were in the water. He didn't have any answers. Could he save them? He'd done it twice already. How big could a Kraken really be? "Scatter," he said. "Don't float on the surface, or it'll see you against the sky like a carp coming up for a fat bug. Go down and lie on the bottom and don't move a muscle." Jack heaved his helmet forward and scooted after it. "It won't see you very well against the bottom. Breathe slowly and save your air and come up only when you have to. Wait for nightfall."

"What will you do?" Peter said, looking at Jack's legs and knowing he wouldn't be agile in the shallows.

"I'm going deep," Jack said as the water reached his chest and the heavy tank on his back grew lighter. "See if I can't hunt it from underneath."

Eyes widened. "With what? We've no weapons. Nothing."

"History." Jack grinned. "King Randolph's Sixth Regiment was driven into the lake at the end. The shore has to be littered with rusting swords and spears." *And bones*, he thought.

He hefted the dripping brass helmet over his head, winced at the weight on his shoulders, and screwed the air tube into place. The sound of stamping ogres' feet dulled. He looked back through the ear-side window in the helmet and made himself smile one more time. Boys had begun to separate slowly, dragging their gear.

Jack scooted forward one push at a time, his helmet and the lead weights on his belt keeping him pressed to the mud. In no time he slid under the surface, moving gently to keep from making waves or letting his helmet fill with water. He was not a fish and found the waterline rising across his helmet windows supremely uncomfortable, especially with the Kraken lurking. He watched the gauge on his air tank warily as it dropped. He needed to move faster.

At about five or six feet deep, he passed the first rusted armor. Some chestpieces remained intact, lying near greaves and vambraces. Those soldiers must have drowned. Other pieces of armor were crushed and scattered. Swords and spears were plentiful, rusted and missing their grips. They would do for lack of anything else, so he took a short, heavy blade and held it by the rusted tang where the grip used to be.

Out past the scattered remnants of that final, desperate battle, deeper and deeper, the water grew cold. Jack didn't know how deep he was now, but the light of the surface shimmered brightly far above him. He could only hear his own rasping breath, and he tried to slow it to save air.

With a sudden jerk he slipped on the steep, mucky slope and slid into the blackness for several terrifying seconds, imagining himself falling straight into the maw of the kraken as it rose to meet him. With a skidding thud he caught up against a gravellier surface, coming to rest at an awkward angle. He had no idea where the sword had gone in the fall. He held perfectly still while the weight of water lay like an anvil on his chest. It was hard to tell, but he thought his air-gauge showed the tank half empty. That slip might have doomed him. Under the weight of his helmet and tank, and with his legs, he didn't know how he'd get back.

Panic rose for the first time, and frustrated helplessness. There was nothing he hated more than feeling helpless. He felt the walls of his helmet closing in. He'd have to drop it and swim for the surface as fast as his arms could take him.

His breath caught as a black shape passed across the gloom above him to blot out the sky and kept passing. His fingers dug into the freezing mud. That was the kraken? He'd never seen anything so big. And they were expected to fight it? Or even survive it? No, no they weren't.

But as the kraken cast him in its shadow, Jack saw a glow below him, a feeble gleam lost in the returning light as the beast passed. Could the kraken be safeguarding something?

Quickly, he scooted again, sliding further down the steep slope, dropping several feet and fetching up again and again. He labored to breathe, but the glow swelled brighter and bigger. He reached the flat bottom of the lake, knocking up a cloud of silt and last year's dead leaves that hung in the water like fog. But he could see the *house*.

It was a grand, sprawling house, built in the style of the country lord who governed Jack's village. Warm light poured from the many windows, and the front doors stood open.

Could the weight of water, the cold, the failing air, be playing tricks on his mind?

He scooted frantically, trying to keep that desperately comforting image centered in the forward window of his helmet. Doors of light. He pulled himself up the front steps with cold-numb hands. His air-gauge read close to empty as he passed into diffuse light from cold gloom. A flooded entry vestibule; a small, close room with a bright ceiling; a ladder on the wall. Focused on his cramped hands, Jack climbed the red-rusted iron rungs. The little window of his heavy helmet broke the surface. Air. The bright ceiling proved to be a surface of water in the floor of another vestibule—wider and warmer.

Jack shoved his helmet off and swung it up onto the floor, gasping, panting, clinging to the ladder. He couldn't understand where he was, but he felt alive. And for the first time he realized he wanted to live. All those times before, fighting the ogres, it hadn't seemed real. But here... it wasn't possible to imagine beating the kraken or the crushing weight of water or dwindling air. Somewhere above, his newfound comrades were dying, and a vast gulf separated them all.

He shrugged out of his air tank and hung it from the top of the ladder, followed by his weight-belt. Then he floundered up onto the wooden floor, streaming water from his clothes and hair and shivering uncontrollably. He couldn't move as a beautiful, young woman opened the door, shrieked in surprise, and closed the door again. A bolt-lock slammed home. Nor could he move a short while later as the door opened again and four royal guardsmen, each wearing the colors of different kingdoms, came through and hefted him up by the arms and legs. They carried him, dripping water, through sumptuous room after sumptuous room until they lowered him to a luxuriant, bearskin carpet before an ornate steam radiator that oozed life-giving heat.

Jack couldn't think. He couldn't stop shivering, but slowly his muscles relaxed until he could roll over. Six women perched on couches and settees stared at him silently. Six royal guards in a complement of colors stood at attention behind them, spears held high.

He glanced around. Tapestries hung on solid walls. Candles burned everywhere, augmented by mirrors. Dark windows looked out into darker water. The ceiling was painted blue like the sky.

"Where am I?" he rasped.

Bodies stirred and dresses rustled across the room as the women shifted. One of the six leaned forward.

"You are in the Troll King's palace at the bottom of the lake. We are the daughters of the kings of the six kingdoms, imprisoned with valets and tutors and guards. We are a sizeable household down here. I am Princess Brudhilm."

Jack stared at her, confused. Red hair cascaded down around a freckled, pale face. "Princesses?" he stammered.

She laughed. "As if that title were worth anything. Our brothers, the princes, are held in another prison. And who are you?"

Jack flopped his head back on the rug. "I am lost, Princess. Princesses. For two days I have fought and matched the king's ogres. Today… who can fight a kraken? I descended, rather than die in the shallows and sun. I am Jack, eldest son of Marrylon of Village Sacksmin in Taurriggen." He nodded to the princess in Taurriggen-blue and the guard behind her. "But what does it matter now? I'm one more dead boy in the Troll King's games." He'd never see his family again.

Again the stir of bodies, concern and grief painted across their faces. Princess Brudhilm shook her head. "You must be brave and quick to have matched the ogres." She glanced down at his legs, though it was obvious she was trying not to.

Jack smiled. They didn't bother him today. They had brought him this far, to this fantastical house of water and beauty. Who could ask more of their legs? "Some would say I'm foolhardy," he said, "though brave sounds nicer. And I'm only quick while wearing the king's armor. Down here I have no speed or weapons."

Princess Brudhilm stood, smoothing her sunshine-yellow dress across her hips. "The kraken's eyes are on the top of its head, and its belly is soft and unprotected. If he had a spear, be he foolhardy or brave, a man could do some terrible damage." She glanced at the guards arrayed around the room. "And I think six foolhardy and brave men alongside you could do even more. Perhaps even kill the beast."

Jack sat up as the six guardsmen gripped their spears tighter, eagerness flooding their faces. Their princess-wards had turned on their seats to look up at their men in concern, but also with determination.

"But," Jack said, his heart beating the same frightened drumbeat it had hammered out over the past few days, "if you could have killed it before, why didn't you?"

"You have to know where the beast is," Princess Brudhilm said, "and it needs to be distracted. Usually, they drive eight or ten cows into the lake when the Troll King wants to bring us up. Besides, even if we were to kill it, there are still his ogres."

"Yes, the ogres," Jack nodded. He rubbed his eyes, picturing the beasts in their armor. The scores around the lake were only a part of the Troll King's army.

"That's where you come in," Princess Brudhilm said.

Jack's eyes snapped open. "Me?"

"If you win the games, there'll be a celebration. Everyone will be there. You could get close to the Troll King."

"Close doesn't help when he can't be killed."

"He's not immortal, he's just taken his heart out and hidden it somewhere. It'll be close to him. My aunt told me, just before he killed her, that he doesn't like to let it out of his sight for long. He keeps moving it. If you can find it, you can leap forward and stab it."

"With all due respect, Your Highness, I don't leap."

She frowned with genuine sadness. "Chances like this are rare. No one has gotten so close to the king since my aunt. You can and you must."

"Princess, I will humbly do my best, foolhardy as I am, but you might want a backup plan."

"There is no backup plan, and I will be eternally grateful for anything you can do."

Jack felt himself blushing fiercely. Everyone was looking at him. Beautiful women, princesses, were looking at him in the same way the boys, the eldest sons, had looked at him. Desperate.

He had dreamed of this so many times, though he would never have admitted it. Running with the boys, earning their respect, besting them even. Sitting with pretty girls, talking with them, seeing in their eyes that they knew he was really there. These moments had awakened a yearning in him that was as painful as the constant fear of dying.

"You don't owe me anything," he mumbled to Princess Brudhilm.

She approached and knelt at his side, taking his hand. "Of course I do." Her hand felt small and smooth as a river stone in his large, calloused, farm-boy hand. "But now you have to go. The king will notice if you stay down here much longer on one tank of air."

He shook his head, looking down at his feet. "I can't climb the mud."

"Our men will carry you."

"No one carries me!"

"Then you die, and this chance dies with you. Would you ride a horse?"

"I guess." He wouldn't admit that he'd never ridden a horse before.

"People ride horses to go faster and farther than their legs can carry them. You will be carried for the same reason." Her voice softened. "Don't make me command you."

He squeezed her hand, then looked to the personal guards of the six princesses. "Give me a spear and get your air tanks."

In the end, two guards held Jack under the armpits and dragged him up the black bottom of the lake. The guardsmen all wore double-tanks for the journey up and then back down again. It was murky going and cold, and every little while the small group would halt as a massive shadow passed above them.

It's circling, Jack thought on the third pass. *Hunting*. He prayed the other boys were lying flat and silent in the shallow bottom and began to count heartbeats.

At one hundred and thirty-eight heartbeats, the shadow passed over them again, closer now as they rose into light and warmth. They passed a breathing tank, new and dented, where it had rolled from higher up. Fifty-seven, fifty-eight. His heart beat loud in his ears. Before it came again, Jack motioned everyone to freeze. Right on time the beast swept over their heads, a bare ten feet above, a riot of slick green and undulating arms. Bigger than any animal had a right to be. After it passed, they staggered up a short ways further and dug themselves in on the lake bottom for purchase. Jack propped himself up on his knees, counting and counting, while the king's guards quickly switched hoses to their second tanks. Jack glanced down at his gauge. A little air left, but he knew if he died here, it wouldn't be for lack of air. He held up his hands and ticked away the last ten heartbeats on his fingers.

And then it was on them, a crushing roll of fast-moving strength and darkness. Jack stabbed up hard with his spear, only to be hauled back off his knees and tumbled as the weapon was wrenched from his hands.

His heavy brass helmet filled with water and pulled him down. Panicking, he got his thumbs under the rim and shoved it off, then squirmed out of the useless tank. Desperate, his hands struck sand, and he pushed up as hard as he could, paddling through churning haze toward the light. He broke the surface, coughing and gasping, then pushed his hair from his eyes as a massive tentacle as big around as his waist rose and then crashed down in the water beside him.

He backpaddled quickly as it rose again and swam hard for the shallows twenty feet away. Looking back over his shoulder he could see the kraken on the surface, eyes wild, beaked jaw opening and closing, tentacles writhing. It rolled and Jack saw half a dozen spears jutting up from its belly. Then it submerged and vanished, perhaps back to some lair in darkness to lick its wounds and die.

Whooping cries rose from around the shores of the lake as clusters of boys stood from waist-deep water near and far. Jack grabbed a rusty spear from the bottom and used it to lever himself to his feet. Then he raised it triumphantly over his head.

The cries were taken up by the crowds of spectators. The ogres in their mighty armor at the water's edge stood uncomfortably, snapping their jaws, swinging their maul hammers, clearly unsure of what to do. Jack waved the rusted spear once more, scanning the water behind him for a hint of the princesses' guards who had truly carried the day. Not a ripple broke the surface. If any had died, crushed or drowned, their brethren had taken the bodies back down below.

William splashed into the lake at a run to help Jack walk out. Peter got under his other arm. It was embarrassing, but necessary and made walking in the bloody water possible. The Troll King, bound in scarred, gray battle armor, waited between ogres at the lake's edge, water lapping at the tips of his brass toe-claws.

"How many'd we lose?" Jack whispered.

"I guess maybe half," William whispered back.

Jack flushed cold. He'd saved some, lost many. Is this how generals felt after a battle? Leading men was not something he had experience with, even if he'd dreamed about it, and losing men felt awful. He'd defeated the kraken and failed to protect his comrades.

"Your Majesty," he said. Water dripped from his hair down across his face. He shivered.

"Congratulations, young Jack," the Troll King said with false humor. Jack could see the effort it took for the king to smile. "Perhaps I had the dwarves make your equipment a little too well, eh? Nevertheless, you are the clear winner of this year's solstice. We will have a feast in your honor." He turned to the cheering crowd. "We will have a feast for *all* the valiant survivors."

Back at the castle where doctors once again hovered to bind wounds, Jack was pulled aside into a small room for an examination. His legs shook worse than usual from exhaustion and nerves.

A few minutes later, he was surprised to see William bustle into the room and shoo the doctor out.

"This way, quick," William said, pushing past Jack toward the back of the room and a small door. "Servants' corridor," he said, pointing.

Jack limped after him along a rather narrow corridor of doors. A fair distance down, William knocked on one of the doors and then yanked it open. A rumbling of voices spilled out and then fell silent. Jack stepped up to the open door to see a large storage room of dry goods, and about thirty young men and women packed in and sitting on stacked sacks of grain. William helped lower Jack to a sack while he marveled at the quantity of food in this one room.

In the center of the chamber, in a plain wool dress of light green, waited Lady Castiline. Her long hair was braided tightly back revealing her long face and thin lips.

"This is it, then," William said excitedly, striding to stand beside her and spreading his arms wide. "Against all odds you survived the tournament, a lot of boys survived the tournament, and tonight we take back the kingdoms."

Lady Castiline stared at Jack, and he grew uncomfortable. The beautiful princesses had stared at him out of desperation and hope. This beautiful woman was staring at him in a much more measured fashion, and he felt he needed to prove himself to her.

"He knows the suits of armor were stolen," Jack said, guessing these people were the heart of the rebellion. There weren't any older people here—not a single person who was alive when the Troll King defeated King Randolph's armies. No one who remembered what it was like. "He's waiting for you."

"He's arrogant," William said fiercely. "He won't bother taking precautions against us."

"Should he?"

"Damned right, he should. We've been practicing for years in human-forged armor. These people here are the best armor-riders we have, and the dwarf-made armor we stole is a thousand times better than anything we've been able to make."

"The close quarters inside the castle work in our favor," Lady Castiline said. "The ogres can't hit us from the air or leap over us. We're smaller and faster than they are."

"Close quarters brings you right under their maul hammers," Jack countered.

"Not *that* close," William interrupted. "We're going to copy what you did and keep one arm free with a spear. Try to hold some distance away from the maul hammers until we can break their steam hoses. We practiced yesterday in the storage cellars."

Jack closed his eyes, picturing it. Picturing the ogres in the main corridors of the castle. "You won't be able to hold your separation indoors. They'll crowd you. Push each other from behind until nobody has space to move. Once they smell blood, they lose control."

"What do you think we should do, then," Lady Castiline said softly, still staring. "We've got bowmen, but arrows barely get through ogre hide."

"Breaking their steam hoses will drop them to their knees. You can use their frozen armor like a shield, blocking others."

"That close, our legs would get tangled," William said. "It's not like dancing — we can't pivot on such big feet."

"Welcome to my world."

William grimaced with irritation.

"Look," Jack said, sitting up straighter and rubbing cramped muscles in his right thigh, "Lady Castiline's right — close quarters will be your advantage. They'll swarm but they can't swing their maul hammers once they get close. And when I say close, I mean really tight. If you can't get behind them, the only way at the back hoses is to step in close, take the first hit, and reach around them. Maybe with a hook instead of the spear."

Heads around the room shook emphatically.

"There's no way our armor'll withstand a single strike from a maul hammer," Lady Castiline said. Her gaze was farther away now, looking into the distance.

"Mount shields," Jack said, "like the knights did, only sized bigger for your armor. Something that can take one hit and hold, because that's all you'll need."

"Even if we find enough metal for shields," said another young man, "we'll get knocked over. Have you seen those hammers? We'll end up flat on our backs, laid out for a second hammer swing."

"Yes, I've seen the maul hammers," Jack said dryly. "Closer than I'd like. You'll have to pair up. The rear person will brace the first and keep them from falling. The front person holds the hook to grapple steam hoses."

Nauseous looks on faces told Jack that these ambitious lords and ladies were suddenly realizing how ugly it was about to get, and how unlike their furtive training combat. This would be metal to metal, chest to chest, teeth to teeth.

But Lady Castiline looked pleased. She focused her eyes on Jack again, but this time the fierce appraisal was gone. He had passed some test, and he was happy. "We can make this work."

Jack nodded to her. "I'll distract the king." He knew he'd doomed himself by linking with the rebellion. He'd survived three long days, only to die anyway in the end.

"Distract him how?" William said.

Jack spun his staff in his hands, feeling the smooth patches of wood where he always gripped. "The same as you. I'll get in close and take the hit. It's the only way."

The grand hall was still dwarfing and cold, even with so many people in the galleries celebrating Jack's victory.

The tables that had once been set for forty-seven were set again, though only eighteen battered and broken combatants had survived all three days. By unspoken consensus, the boys all huddled together at the first two tables, trying to accommodate splints and bandages. Eyes were red from exhaustion. Jack sat at their head.

It was a seat he had earned, but he felt vulnerable. His fellow survivors all looked to him for leadership. He missed the safety of being at the rear.

The galleries above were crowded and raucous. Music poured down from dozens of minstrels competing with each other. Jack barely tasted the rich feast before him, struggling not to glance around. Everyone watched the room closely, despite the gaiety. This was it. Thirty men and women in armor against scores of ogres. The revolution would begin and end here today. Were people still taking bets?

The Troll King was the key. He was the will that held the ogres together and without him, they were simply raging beasts. Organized or not, they were terrifying. The rebels in armor couldn't last long unless Jack did something.

The Troll King sat before them all on his oversized throne, built for the armor he wore to protect his weak body, behind a carved table bearing platters of sumptuous food that he did not touch. His small eyes flicked back and forth between Jack and the galleries above. The six captive kings were arrayed behind him on their lesser thrones with their queens at their side today. Did they know? Had their daughters at the bottom of the lake gotten them any information? Ogres stood behind them, possibly to prevent sudden acts of bravery. Was the king finally growing cautious?

The king stood with a rattle and silence fell in stages across the room until everything fell still. Jack could hear the soft wheeze of steam as the king's pistons locked into the upright position, and the occasional splash from the raised pond beside him. The ogres along the walls creaked and banged as they stood up, stretching their brass-and-iron rooster legs tall. Maul hammers swung lazily. Jack could feel the tension in the room, thick and eager, still masked by pleasantries.

"To the victor!" shouted the Troll King, hefting a mighty tankard of ale in his metal-armor fist, sloshing half of the contents to the floor.

The crowd cheered and wine glasses rose in toast. The Troll King put his tankard back on the table without drinking and waived Jack forward, finger-knives clicking. Jack stood with the help of his staff. Now it was his turn before the crowd, the most terrifying place he could imagine.

Once standing, his tired and aching legs wouldn't cooperate, and he struggled to get them free of the bench. Peter offered a hand and Jack almost refused by habit, but then he gripped the hand held out to him. He couldn't let himself fall on his face, not now. His heart drummed and cold sweat ran down his spine. Everyone stared at him.

He took one step free of the table and then another, leaning hard on the staff. He needed his legs to work, and he had taxed them over the past few days. Not just his legs—his arms and stomach ached. The blisters on his arm were still raw from the steam hoses on the first day and his body was bruised from the kraken, but he needed to get close to the Troll King. Where could the heart be hidden? The hall was so vast and so empty there didn't seem to be any obvious spots. There were a few iron and copper boxes hung from the king's armor itself, but why would he bother to take it out only to hide it on his person?

Jack's eyes were drawn up to the skins stretched on the wall high above. Arch King Randolph and his six lesser kings. Many of his children were up there, though people often spoke of his two daughters who had escaped to foreign lands. He glanced back at the bruised faces of the boys behind him. They'd followed him on that last day and survived, some of them. They would follow him today—they had a small part to play. He turned back to the king and forced himself into the emptiness while everyone looked on, his shuffling footsteps echoing harshly, grit against aged flagstones, and the thump of his staff.

The silence stretched and he could faintly hear water bubbling in the boilers on the ogres' backs. Hear his own labored breathing. It still struck him as odd that such a vast space could be indoors, void of sunlight and birdsong.

It also struck him as odd that everyone could know what was about to happen and no one said a thing.

The Troll King broke the silence first. "Did you enjoy my lake, Jack?"

"Yes, Your Majesty." Jack kept his eyes at the king's feet. "I've often looked down at fish through the surface of the water. I've never looked up at one."

"That was an impressive feat, placing six spears in the kraken's belly at once."

"That was luck, and the movement of the beast over the top of me. I expected to drown, but instead I was nearly crushed to death."

"I like you," the king said, and his voice sounded wistful. "You were ruthless when you needed to be and never hesitated. I had hoped you would win."

"Thank you, Your Majesty. I was hoping I'd survive."

"You don't like me much, do you?"

"I got to experience wonders beyond dreams." Jack lifted his eyes to the Troll King's. "I imagine the boys who died have greater complaint."

"Hah! I'll miss that sharp tongue." The king took a step forward, a crack of brass on stone that echoed across the room and looked pointedly up at the waiting galleries.

"You have won gold enough for ten lifetimes. Take your prize and go, young Jack, or you won't be able to outrun this fight. That is my boon to you for winning the solstice competition. Run away home."

"I can't go."

"Think carefully on your choice. You are just one man, a *boy*, and you are nothing without armor. My ogres have killed a thousand men just like you."

"I know."

Doors at the side of the hall beneath the galleys swung open, but it wasn't with the bang Jack had been expecting. Six doors in a row opened smoothly, held wide by six men and women with black hoods pulled low over their faces. The silence in the room stretched several heartbeats, Jack and the Troll King both turned to face the doors, and then came the unmistakable clacking booms of brass-and-iron feet on stone.

William and his crew had to hunch deeply on their rooster legs to get through the doors, and Jack immediately saw why as the first six straightened in stolen armor. Their left piston-arms were bent up and over awkwardly, and slabs of curved metal that looked like halves of boilers had been attached across the shoulder and down to the forearm. Long hooks were fixed to the backs of their right hands.

"Goodbye, young Jack," the Troll King said without turning, his eyes locked on the young lords and ladies who defied him. "It was lovely meeting you."

With a howling roar, the ogres along the walls erupted into a pushing and shoving mob of armored eagerness, striving to be first into the fight. Some fell. Enough fought clear and broke into a crashing lope across flagstones, crossing the expanse of the hall in seconds as six more armored humans clambered through the doors and leaned into the backs of their front line. The ogres didn't slow, and hundreds of pounds of metal and flesh and rage struck down the shields with maul hammers as thick around as a man's waist. Knees buckled and armor foundered in a sickening crash. Boiler-plating shields shattered and steam pistons in raised arms collapsed.

But Jack had been right. The armor and shields only had to withstand one hit. Hook-hands lashed out around ogres too crowded to recover for a second swing and hoses burst, spewing steam across the unprotected faces and chests of ogres tight behind. Front ogres folded up in their now-useless armor, forming a frozen bulwark between the badly injured front lords before them and the flailing, raging, steam-burned beasts behind. More lords and ladies pushed through the doors with hooks and spears to reach over the heads of the fallen ogres, and arrows began to rain down from the galleries into the bunched masses.

"Go!" Jack bellowed, waving at Peter and the boys he'd left behind at the tables.

Those who could run headed for the grand doors to bolt them before the vast numbers of ogres outside heard the tumult and joined in. Those boys who couldn't run hobbled for safety.

The Troll King was shouting and trying to regain order. More than a dozen ogres appeared to be down with detached steam hoses, hunched on the floor in frozen armor, but most of the lords and ladies on the front line had not gotten up either. More arrows rained down now as ladies in the galleries untangled bows from amidst their flowing dresses, but the arrows barely penetrated thick ogre hides. There were screams and shouts; cursing. Someone fell from the galleries.

Snarling ogres moved among the upper revelers now. More screams, more people falling or tossed. Jack turned to the end of the hall where all six lesser thrones stood empty, the human kings and their children had fled.

He set out, skirting the battle, alone and happier without everyone watching him. The wounded and furious bellowing of ogres was terrifying as they pushed against the resolute core of rebels like waves pounding a riverbank. The Troll King pulled ogres from the back of the pack, organizing them for a proper attack. There wasn't much time. Jack needed to find the hidden heart.

Among the thrones now, through scattered food and one fur-lined shoe on its side, Jack searched, finding nothing. Everything was sparse, desolate and cold. Except... the little fishpond? The king loved his fish — until he ate them.

Steadying himself on the edge of the king's huge throne, gouged and scratched from armor, Jack hefted his staff and stabbed it down at one of the large coy beneath the shallow water. The head of his staff hit home, and the fish twisted and struggled away, obviously wounded. Jack looked at the Troll King. Nothing. He targeted another fish, and then another. There was blood in the water now, and one of the fish rose to the surface on its side, flipping weakly. He struck three more fish before suddenly hearing a high-pitched shriek from across the room. An instant later the sound of metal feet striking the flagstones, rapidly approaching.

Jack let himself fall to the floor as he grabbed the last fish, a particularly large coy with elegant gold blotches across its back and a white belly. He flipped it out of the water and snatched up a fallen dinner knife. Slitting open the fish's stomach, a chestnut-colored lump fell free, pulsing and throbbing. The king's heart. Jack snatched at it just as a fist of finger-knives the size of his head struck him across the chest, lifting him off of the floor and throwing him a dozen paces. Ribs broke.

The Troll King glared furiously, armored feet straddling the gnarled, beating heart on the floor. Two arrows jutted from his side, rising and falling as he breathed.

"I toasted you only minutes ago," the king called over the cacophony behind him. "You throw hospitality in my face?"

A fire had broken out on the third tier of the galleries, spreading along wall tapestries. Most of the bowmen and women had exhausted their arrows and fled, while William's armored rebels were being pushed back toward the doors, though they remained somewhat protected by husks of broken armor in the way.

"How are you going to pick it up," Jack called back, then gasped at the tearing pain in his broken ribs.

The Troll King began to unbuckle straps. "I fear nothing," he muttered.

Jack didn't think he could stand, but he fought the pain and pulled himself up with his staff and the help of a nearby throne.

"So what now, Your Majesty?" he called.

The king climbed down the leg of his armor, looking frail and spindly without his augmented metal. He stepped to the floor and yanked the two arrows out of his side, tossing them aside. "Your skin will join those up on my wall," he said.

He never took his eyes from Jack's as he crouched down between his armor's feet and gently lifted his heart; then he swallowed it whole. Grinning darkly, he swung back up onto his armor's leg and scampered up the structure.

Jack hefted his staff and threw it like a spear. He had an image in his head of running the king through and pinning him to his armor, but the blunt-ended staff simply struck the king between the shoulder blades and bounced him back to the floor, cracking his head on stone.

Jack lunged forward, staggering across the space between them as the king writhed, and half fell on top of the troll. The dinner knife he'd used to gut the fish was still at hand and he grabbed it as he coughed up blood.

"Wait," the king shouted, raising his hands.

Jack drove the blade into the king's stomach where he knew the heart to be at the moment, then he stood slowly as the king gagged and choked and fell silent. The ogres still fought with fury.

Jack tugged at the buckles of the feet on the king's armor and pulled the footplates down, lightheaded from pain. Then he used the king's throne to climb up the mechanism and into the seat, strapping his legs in and lengthening the arms. The inside of the armor stank of troll.

Holding his breath against grinding ribs, with no staff, just a modest cudgel at the end of one arm and finger-knives on the other, Jack moved against the rear of the straining ogre-pack. He yanked or cut eight hoses before they even realized he was a threat, but that was all the luck he was allowed. A ninth ogre turned and swung its maul hammer backhanded. Jack evaded the hit and stepped in close, stabbing finger-knives into the ogre's vulnerable stomach with steam-driven strength, but he was not able to duck the strike of the next ogre in the line or the one beyond that one. He went sprawling, his ears ringing and his ribs in agony. The king's extraordinary armor crumpled but did not collapse.

There was fighting all around him now, more than there should have been. Jack tried to focus. Was that Peter? In armor? Had they gone for the remaining suits in the armory? It wasn't just Peter and a few other boys from the solstice games, there were a lot of people fighting. Some of the armor was rough iron, bulky and slow, but powerful. The tide was turning. Ogres' armor seized-up as the rebels used every opportunity to break hoses rather than engage.

Jack slowly pushed himself to his feet. The king's armor canted to the left now and the hip didn't rotate smoothly, but it could move. A shadow fell over him and a woman marched past in a suit of black-iron armor that dwarfed even the ogres' massive size. He recognized Lady Castiline's braid. The boiler on her back was as big as a wagon, and her fists were iron balls to match the maul hammers. The Troll King's armor barely came up to her chest. Flagstones cracked under her tread. Apparently, they had been experimenting with size rather than agility in their backroom smithies, and she alone carved a path through the center of the ogre pack to ease the pressure on William's crippled line, smashing ogres right and left.

Jack fell in close behind her, protecting her back, cleaning up after her, yanking hoses off the ogres she struck to make sure they stayed down. Ogres began to fall back across the hall, perhaps finally realizing they were outmatched. Space cleared near the doors where the battle had begun.

"You look a mess," Jack called down to William. William's shield had buckled and bent around his collapsed left arm, ground up into the side of his armor. The hook on his right hand was stretched out, twisted and bloody. He was bloody. Blood ran down the side of his face from a head wound, and crushed armor pinned his arm. He was panting hard. They all were, the spearmen behind and the crippled front line. A dozen armored people sprawled on the floor, unmoving. Lady Castiline bashed aside half a dozen ogres in frozen armor to clear the area.

"Did we win?" William wheezed; his eyes pained.

"Almost. King's dead. We just have to deal with the hundreds of ogres outside." Jack looked up at Lady Castiline above him. She had a gouge across her cheek and one of her eyebrows was singed off. This was not her first suit of armor tonight. "Come with me," he called up.

He turned and tromped across the wide hall toward the cluster of ogres trying to organize into a defensive square. There were perhaps forty left. Just behind him, clearly audible over his own cracking footsteps, thumped Lady Castiline. The human defenders, battered and showing a lot more damage than their ogre enemies, followed after them *en masse*.

"Listen to me," Jack bellowed. "Your king is dead. The castle is lost." He gestured to Lady Castiline with his clacking finger-knives. "And we have an army of a thousand of these coming up from the cellars. If you climb out of your armor right now, you may leave. If not, you will be crushed to death. Leave this castle and leave our kingdoms. Go back to your homes."

He fell silent. Lady Castiline whispered, "We only have one. We can't keep the steam pressure up high enough to move it, so we keep blowing seals. It's going to break down any moment."

Jack looked at her and gave her a grin as fearful ogres began to unbuckle straps and harnesses and climb gingerly to the floor. "One is enough."

Ice-Locked Off Hatter's Island

Captain Stephen Passruck pulled his hood lower over his face against the howling arctic wind, eyes watering, struggling to drag a laden sled of coal over the hardpacked snow and ice, one foot in front of the other. It had to be fifty below, if it was a degree, and he couldn't feel his fingers on the windward side. He wore many layers, the whole rescue expedition did — polar bear fur and wolf fur and wool and leather — but this three-day storm was chewing on them. Day and night, the wind poured down from the north, flowing between ice-clad, rocky islands and battering the tiny people who dared defy the frozen ocean in late winter.

His best mates, Randolph Katrain and Big Annie Anden, staggered at his side, along with twenty of His Majesty's soldiers and twenty native ice-dwellers that they'd hired to guide and help drag food and tons of coal.

Stephen refused to stop. He'd left the steamship *Butterfall* nearly four months ago, trapped in ice. He and a dozen others had slogged three hundred miles south to the nearest trading station to send word of the situation to the Company and gather additional supplies and help.

He was going to reach the *Butterfall,* and he was going to rescue the one thousand, five hundred refugees on board.

The cold had come unusually early this year, and the *Butterfall* left Slaugiss loaded with people unusually late in the season. Everything that could go wrong had, and they'd been forced to break through new-forming ice for weeks, paddlewheels churning, making for the southlands. It was a futile race, and the effort of icebreaking had burned through their coal supplies three hundred miles short of their destination. The boilers grew cold, and they'd gotten locked in about a quarter mile out from a lone mountain called Hatter's Island, a solitary block of granite and snow that thrust up from the ocean's depths. It was the last of a string of towering seamounts in this archipelago of ice.

Stephen had stayed with the ship for several weeks. He and the crew had established an emergency basecamp on the only low slope of Hatter's Island that met the sea and brought some supplies over as a precaution in case the ship got crushed under the pressure of shifting ice. There was enough food for six months, plenty for the passengers, plus coats and blankets. His second in command, Albert Brice, remained behind to oversee the ship and passengers. *Albert is a good man,* Stephen thought. *He'll have kept them alive.*

He squinted through the growing daylight. Two mountains reared up in the distance—Maycomb Island and then Hatter's beyond it, according to maps and Stephen's own pencil notations from the hard journey south. The local ice-dwellers who were helping with the rescue called Hatter's Island *"Ma'rab"*, or 'dark beast' in their tongue. They advised against anyone stepping on its beach as they'd had a summer fishing village there in ancient times that had vanished. They would not go beyond Maycomb Island on this mission, but they'd brought the party close enough.

Stephen tugged a pocket watch from under his coat and peered at it. Ten in the morning. The sun should just clear the horizon by around eleven and then set two hours later. Everyone's mood rose and fell with its anemic rays.

It took the rest of the day of exhausted dragging and frequent rests to reach the massive lee of Maycomb Island. The peak blocked the driving wind, but it continued to swirl and gust as it spun off the mountain. The rescue party established camp on a gravel beachhead, and Stephen ordered the cooks to start up fires and prepare a hearty meal. The light and heat from the coal fires were much appreciated in the polar night as forty sleds of coal bound in canvas were tied down in rows on the ice.

"I can't stay," he said to Annie, arms crossed, watching the bustle from a rise above the rocky beach. He looked across the next ice-gap to Hatter's Island and could only just make it out. There were no lights shining back. The *Butterfall* emergency camp was around a north bend out of sight, but he doubted anyone manned it.

Annie turned to him, dark, glittering eyes peering out of her fur-lined hood. The starlight glowed bright on the ice, enough to see by. "It's going to be another slog," she called back over the whining, mumbling wind. "Probably several hours. I know you're anxious, I am too, but you should rest and warm up. Get food in you."

"I can't." Stephen pulled out his watch again. Eight in the evening. He returned his gaze to the distant mountain's silhouette. "I'll go by myself. If I can get to them, at least they'll know someone's here."

"Let's gather a small group and drag one or two sleds together. Numbers are safer against polar bears. If we find the ship, we'll get the boilers fired up and give them heat."

Stephen looked at her and smiled, feeling the weight of exhaustion and worry. He needed to know the stranded people were all right. "We'll heat the boilers slowly. The water in the tanks is frozen solid, and we can't afford to burst pipes."

They ate at Annie's sensible insistence, and then a party of six assembled on the beach. They prepared two sleds, one of coal and one of supplies and blankets and food. Stephen, Big Annie, and Randolph were joined by three guardsmen of impressive size, and they all carried long guns strapped to their backs to fend off polar bears. Attacks had been semi-regular on the journey north, particularly around the islands where seals gathered.

The ice-dwellers watched them with tense nervousness.

"Be careful over there," the group's leader, Andack, whispered urgently as they worked to split the sled harness into multiple traces for multiple people. "That island is cursed. You don't know what you'll find."

Stephen took the man's gloved hand in his. "We'll be careful."

Andack frowned. "Ships go missing near there."

"What do your stories say?" Stephen asked.

"It was a long time ago, hundreds of summers ago. The camp of our ancestors had been on that island for many years. Then one day, a young chief named Hallana discovered a terrible beast that had risen up from the depths and crawled onto the island." Andack shuddered. "It was sick, probably dying, but Hallana witnessed it and was cursed with madness. He slew many in the summer camp. Women and children. The returning hunters in their boats, crazed by grief, chased Hallana, but he escaped. We do not sail near there lest we disturb the beast's bones or Hallana's spirit."

"What did this thing look like?"

Andack frowned. "It can't be described. Men's minds break when they see it."

"That's not helpful."

"Tolok is a fallen god, thrown down into the depths of the sea by other gods."

"Why fear it if it's dead, then?"

"Don't dismiss the danger." Andack's gravelly voice dropped. "Tolok has many faces and bodies, and Gods don't die, even when they do. If it comes near, look away."

"We'll be careful." Stephen slipped into a harness, his mind already elsewhere. Every now and then, a steamship through the summer arctic would see something breach that was hard to explain, but Stephen rarely paid the stories any mind. He'd seen giant whales bigger than any tale; he'd seen immense bones on rocky beaches, and they were just animals. Nothing to drive you mad. The ice-dwellers were too superstitious.

He looked at his watch again. Nine o'clock. He craved sleep, though he'd been having strange nightmares for the last few days.

"We'll get 'em home safe." Randolph clapped Stephen on the shoulder.

Stephen nodded, then nodded over to the captain leading the second sled. Both groups began forward, leaving the lee of Maycomb's peak and entering the relentless wind of the open ice once more, sled runners grinding. Stephen breathed slowly to avoid freezing his lungs. His eyes watered, and the tears froze to his lashes.

No one spoke, each bound up in their thoughts. Stephen's were entirely focused on the approaching reality of Hatter's Island — its high, granite mountain just a hollow against the brilliant polar stars. The immensity of the wasteland around them frightened him in a way that he hadn't been frightened for the last four months. All that time, he'd been so focused on going south to the outpost and getting back that he hadn't allowed himself time for fear. Now he was here, counting hours. All that gray uncertainty would be resolved in an instant.

He looked back. The campfires at the foot of Maycomb were small, already far away and yet comforting. The fires meant they weren't alone.

By his pocket watch, it was nearing eleven when they finally entered the wind-shadow of Hatter's Mountain. There was no watchfire to greet them and break the darkness, though Stephen wasn't surprised. Albert wouldn't have wasted precious wood maintaining a fire on the island. If the *Butterfall* was intact, the passengers would be holed up there with what heat they could make.

Shaking his head, he pressed on. The two teams marched along Hatter's' rocky coast where broken ice had piled up, and the mountain loomed above them. Finally, they reached the shallow cove and its beach of tumbled, rounded rocks where the original camp had been made.

"Here," Stephen called. "The camp was here."

They turned together into the cove, dragging their sleds onto land.

As they freed themselves from the harnesses, Randolph nudged Stephen. "Go. Check. I know you're dying to see, but don't get your hopes up."

"I know." Stephen hurried across the beach, exhausted legs burning, coughing from cold, and clambered up the short, steep embankment to the hard-frozen ground of the mountain's lowest slope. Big Annie joined him at an old fire pit and three half-collapsed tents. One of the soldiers joined them, rifle at ready.

"These are empty," Stephen said, kicking at the stacked, wooden crates tangled up in the tents. "They took the supplies back to the ship."

"Then the ship must be nearby."

Stephen crouched at the firepit and picked up a sliver of burnt crate board, then they both turned back to the ice.

"The icefloe stops and starts," Stephen said quietly. He sniffed the wood. The char-smell was old, nearly dead. "The ship might be right in front of us, or she could be miles away at the whim of the flow."

"Well, we're not finding her in the dark, Stephen. Wait for the noon-sun tomorrow and search while it's light. Be patient."

"Let's make camp." He tossed the bit of board aside. "We'll burn coal. If they're out there, they'll see us."

"Stephen!" Randolph roared from down from the beach. "Come here."

Stephen and Annie clambered down to the treacherous, shifting stones of the beach and hurried as best they were able to their companions. Randolph stood with the captain while the third soldier stood a dozen yards farther along.

"What is it?"

Randolph nodded down at the ground. "Graves. A lot of them."

Stephen choked a cry and staggered forward. He could now see six-foot-long mounds of stones everywhere. The captain kicked at one near him and it partially collapsed with a clatter. A woman's frozen arm lay exposed. He told himself there were bound to be deaths, but guilt gnawed at him.

"They can't have starved," Stephen said when he'd regained his composure.

"Sickness?" Randolph asked. "Scurvy?" He kicked the mound again, and the stones collapsed exposing her head and a gunshot wound to the temple. "Or bullets."

"Bullets?" Stephen turned to the frozen sea. Where was the ship?

"I count forty-two," called the soldier down the beach.

"Forty-two. Damn. Alright, let's set up camp and build a fire. Up above." Away from the brooding dead.

Far south, the moon lifted a bare edge above the horizon, a bright glow that didn't illuminate a thing. Stephen imagined the faint light shimmering across the immense bones of some long-dead sea monster. He shook his head to clear it of fairytales. If there ever were bones, they were long gone.

Gathering at the sleds and untying supplies, they began erecting new tents beside the old ones. No one spoke, and no one touched the old supplies. The soldiers carried up bundles of coal and built a large fire in the pit. A beacon for anyone watching from the wasteland.

Between the cold and the corpses, they slept poorly, and Stephen wrestled with nameless horrors in his dreams. There was always a guard on duty against polar bears, and they took turns with a rifle across their laps beside the fire, but this was the first island they'd been on without a trace of seals, penguins, or bears.

Then sometime in the small hours of the morning, he was awakened by Annie hollering. "A light! A light!"

Fighting blankets, trying to shake off nightmares, Stephen crawled from his tent into the rosy warmth of the fire. Snow had melted in a swath around the firepit, revealing dead grass and dirt.

He joined the others at the edge of the bank, breath streaming out. To the north, maybe a mile out, a small light burned. It had to be the mirrored beacon atop the *Butterfall*.

"They're alive," he said, smiling with relief.

"What time is it?" Randolph asked.

Stephen drew out his pocket watch and squinted at it. The hour hand was moving backward and the minute hand was moving swiftly around the dial. He smacked it several times, then held it to his ear. The restless ticking seemed fast. "Something's wrong with my watch."

"You want to head out there now?"

"Pack up camp."

Within half an hour, the six of them were underway in the darkness, Stephen eagerly pulling forward against the traces, focused on that tiny beacon-light. The *Butterfall* was there. They were *alive*. Most of them, anyway. With so many dead, there must be sickness. Could it be scurvy? He'd brought a crate of onions just in case—that would cure it. But what if it wasn't scurvy?

The ice between the beach and the ship was terribly broken up in many waist-high ridges that had refrozen, so going was slow and exhausting. Stephen checked his watch twice more, but both times the hands were spinning, so he gave up and tucked it away. It had been his grandfather's. Maybe one of the springs was going.

"I see her," Randolph panted after an hour of struggle. The ice groaned and popped around them with its slow flow.

"Where?"

"There. See?"

Stephen squinted at the long, narrow shadow. "Can't be her. That's too far from the beacon."

"Then what is it?"

"Are those masts?"

They'd come more than a mile, but distances were deceptive out on the expanse. Stephen eyed the dark blotch as they dragged the sleds over another ice ridge. The fire they'd left burning on Hatter's Island seemed tiny now.

Another twenty minutes of dragging, and the dark shapes had resolved into three ships. The one with the beacon lay a ways beyond the others.

"A sailing ship?" one of the guards said as they drew close. "How?"

The ice-locked ship was clearly a derelict, gray with age and listing, with all three masts snapped off at various heights. The mast-tops with their tangled spars lay across the deck and down onto the ice. Dry-rotted ropes and remnants of sails swayed in the insistent wind like spiderwebs. Everything creaked and groaned mournfully.

"I haven't seen a three-masted ship since I was a kid," the guard said as they passed along its scarred and splintered side.

"This ship shouldn't be here," Randolph rumbled. "Only the ice is keeping it up. Look at it. How'd it survive the summer thaw? Or the last fifty summers? It can't float."

"Maybe it was beached on the island," Annie said, staring up. "This year's ice could've dragged it back out. What's that structure up on the aft deck?"

"It was a whaler," Stephen said, heart beating fast. Randolph was right, it shouldn't be here. It felt wrong. "That structure's the triworks—the housing where they rendered down the blubber. And see all those empty hoists along the rail? That's where the whaling rowboats would have hung. This is a piece of history."

They passed below the broken bowsprit and around tangled chunks of wood and rope on the ice.

"The *Queen Mandage*," Randolph read off the bow. "Never heard of her. I'll look that up when we get home. See where she was registered, and when she was lost."

Stephen focused on the massive, dark outline of the *Butterfall* in the distance, long and sleek and with twin smokestacks rearing up into the star-studded sky at an uncomfortable tilt. The side-wheel paddles, twenty-eight feet across, were embedded deep in the ice.

"Why don't they have any other lights burning?" Annie said.

"Ahoy!" Stephen called. The crackling ice paused at his shout, then resumed.

"Quiet, you fool," snapped back voices from the darkness. "Hurry!" "Run!"

The six looked at each other and began to hustle. They could not run, the ice was too rough, they were too exhausted, and the air was too cold for heavy breathing, but they came up alongside the tilted hull of the steamship within a few minutes. There were a number of whaler rowboats on the ice beside the steamship, and a crowd of people at the rails in heavy coats bound up against the night. Stephen saw the barrels of rifles pointed out over his head.

Ropes were thrown down with urgency while men clambered down the huge paddles of the sidewheel. No one spoke.

"What's going on?" Stephen demanded as men yanked his harness over his head and those of his companions. They lashed ropes to the sleds, scrambling madly in the dark.

"Quiet." "Get on board." "Quick." "Up the ladder."

Stephen and the others climbed to the main deck as the crowds at the rails above kept rifles steady. Everyone was frighteningly silent. Stephen squinted down the tilted deck. Ten big launchers, with harpoons as tall as a man and thick as an arm, had been mounted at intervals. Crews of three manned every one. They must've taken them from the derelict whaler. It looked like they'd run steam pipes to the launching blocks, but he couldn't be sure as he was hustled past.

Inside, the two-story grand salon was surprisingly light and warm, with the chandeliers above blazing and wall sconces twinkling with tiny flames. The chaos of bustling people halted as they entered, and people crowded the railing of the promenade above, openly staring. Again, no one spoke.

Albert Brice stood waiting in a light coat, grinning, and Stephen pushed back his hood. They embraced, laughing, slapping each other on the back, and Stephen felt how thin his second in command had become. Then Albert hugged Randolph and Annie and nodded to the three guardsmen. He looked far older than when they'd parted four months ago. Gaunt and gray.

"I didn't think you'd make it back," Albert said softly. "Just the six of you, is it?"

"God, no," Stephen said, equally softly, shrugging out of his now-hot coat. "There's over thirty people and forty sleds of coal and supplies camped at Maycomb Island. They'll come over at dawn. What the hell's going on?"

Albert's expression dropped. "They can't. They'll be killed."

"What are you talking about?" Stephen demanded, growing frustrated. Albert turned and hurried aft, and Stephen's group was forced to follow — albeit far more clumsily on the tilted deck. Stephen noted a lack of furniture, and the windows were blacked out with heavy cloth.

Albert stopped beside a table at midships with maps spread across it. Several men and women were gathered there, waiting for them. They were as thin and haggard as Albert. The large map in the center of the table showed the Vaise Archipelago, and Hatter's Island, the northernmost of the seamounts, had been circled. 'X's' had been marked in half a dozen locations around the island.

"Parks," Albert said to a tall man beyond the table.

"You came back," Parks said, eyes flicking excitedly to Stephen and company. Stephen didn't recognize him.

"Forty of them with forty sleds of coal, waiting at Maycomb." Albert stabbed Maycomb Island on the map. "They'll be crossing in the morning. Take someone. Get over there and warn them to stay put. We'll start sending people in twos and threes. Go."

"Albert," Stephen said, "we're waiting here until spring. You can't walk fifteen hundred people all the way to the Cape Vara station."

Albert ignored him and turned to a woman in multiple maroon and red cloaks. "Start prepping the sick and wounded, Mary. The captain's brought two sleds. As soon as we've emptied them of coal, we'll load 'em up with people. Four to a sled, and four to pull 'em. How many are there in sick bay?"

"Forty-seven, at last count."

"We can do it."

"Those ice ridges are terrible to cross," Stephen said. "I've never seen the ice crack and reform in regular lines like that."

Albert nodded. "The four tenders will have to hump the sleds over the ridges as quiet as a mouse."

There was a single shout outside. Heads snapped around, listening. "Start prepping, Mary," Albert said. He ran forward, grabbing a heavy coat. Others were hurrying. Stephen followed.

"You got through because there were only a few of you," Albert called back. He snatched up a rifle and paused at the door as Stephen and Randolph shrugged back into their own coats. "I was hoping they didn't hear you."

"Who?!"

"The beasts."

Outside, the cold hit like a slap after the brief warmth. Everyone stood silent along the rails, rifles up as before, and Stephen and Albert joined them. Randolph and Annie crowded in behind. The beacon light was shuttered now, and Stephen saw his two sleds on the deck, half emptied.

"What…?"

"Shhh," Albert said softly.

Far away, Stephen could see the fire they'd left burning on Hatter's Island still shimmering and wavering. A hard groaning and cracking echoed across the ice.

"They don't know where you are, but they're searching," Albert said under his breath. Abruptly, the fire in the distance vanished, followed a few seconds later by a distant boom. "They don't like fire."

Stephen almost demanded 'Who?' again but froze like a rabbit in lamplight at the sound of distant ice shattering near Hatter's Island. The sound was tremendous, and it was approaching.

"Keep very still," Albert said softly.

The shattering noise raced toward them, then passed north of the *Butterfall* and the derelict whaler. Stephen could just see thick chunks of ice being tossed into the air like toy blocks, then the destruction continued out to sea, fading away.

"They'll be back," Albert said as everyone relaxed, "but we've got a little time." Rifle barrels came up. People began talking softly.

The man from inside, Parks, hurried up with his second man in tow. "We're heading out," he said.

"Step softly," Albert said, clasping the man's arm. "Go with God."

The two men descended the paddlewheel and vanished.

"He's a brave man," Albert said. "He'll get there before morning."

"When's morning, then?" Stephen asked. "My watch stopped working."

"Your watch won't work here, captain. None of them do."

"Are you going to tell us what's going on?"

Albert gestured for them to follow and let them back inside.

"Where did you get fuel?" Stephen said as they peeled off their coats again. "We thought you'd be cold as the tundra in here."

"Have a seat. We saved a few chairs from the fire back in the beginning. I don't have any tea, I'm afraid. We ran out long ago."

"We brought some in the supply crates. You're welcome to it."

"Did you?" Albert seemed delighted and sent someone to hunt for it. They sat in a cluster of wooden chairs on the tilted deck near the map table. "You don't know how happy I am to see you," he said.

"You knew it'd take at least four months to get back here, Albert. We talked about it."

Albert shook his head. "It's been a lot longer than that for us. Time doesn't run straight in here." He stared into the distance. "Just by counting the sun rises and sets, we've been here for over nine months."

"That's not possible," Annie exclaimed.

"It seems longer than that. Things appear, things disappear. Those two ships, for instance. They both appeared one day out of the darkness without a sound. There was a survivor on the whaler, an old man who claimed to have been marooned here sixty years while his crew died one by one. He died from an infection. The other ship was empty. I took the logbooks and maps from the captain's quarters, but I can't read them. I've never seen letters like what's written there, and the sketches?" He shivered. "Another ship appeared, a steamship. The people on board were making too much noise. Before we could quiet them, they got hit by a beast. Breached their hull and left a swath of open water when it passed. The ship was listing, sinking, and the beast circled and dragged the ship below the ice on its second pass."

"You're not making sense."

Albert shrugged. "What do I know about making sense?"

"What are these things, then?" Stephen asked, hands clasped over his belly, eyebrows up. "Whales?"

"Not whales."

"What, then?" Stephen thought back to Andack's story and then the shattering ice. The long lines that had broken and re-frozen. What could do that?

"They're big, that's for sure. It doesn't matter how thick the ice is, they can crack right up through it without a care. And they come up from the blackest depths."

"What do they look like?" one of the guardsmen asked.

Albert shrugged again, looking more uncomfortable. "The things can't really be described; I don't have the words. We've seen them up close a few times, and they can drive you mad if you look too long. Giant squids at one end, I guess. There are pieces of a lot of sea monsters in them. They're maybe a hundred and fifty feet long? Wide around as a ship, and they have bones. Like you just saw with the fire on the island? They can get up onto land if they want to. And the smell…?" He looked up and around. "Intolerable. We killed one early on with harpoons, through luck more than anything. Later, the old whaler showed us how to render the blubber. We got one hundred and seventy-five barrels of oil out of that horror, but no one would dare try the meat. The oil barrels came from the whaler's hold."

"You're using sea monster oil to heat the ship?"

"It's more powerful than coal, though it stinks to high heaven. Stomach-turning. We're trying to keep the burn rate low because… well, nine months is a long time."

The group stirred uncomfortably.

"What about the time, then?" the guard asked. "I can accept sea monsters, there must be things in the sea that we've never seen, but time's fixed."

"Not always. The Company knows about it."

"The Crown and Company have half a dozen spots we're forbidden to steam through," Stephen said. Everyone looked at him. "It's just because sextants and clocks don't work inside them, so navigation's impossible. They say it's a magnetic anomaly. There are certainly no monsters, and everything turns to rights after you make it out. That's not the same as nine months passing in the span of four. Or three-masted ships appearing from of the past."

"And I'm telling you it's true!"

Albert's day-count was clearly off, but Stephen wasn't going to fight him on it. The man had been under a terrible strain. They all had.

Spring always came and ice always broke up and the sun rose to light the world.

"We can't walk the people out," Stephen said.

"Spring's not coming," Albert replied forcefully. "We can't wait. We can walk several hundred people a day while the sun's up. The beasts don't like the sun and Maycomb is beyond their range. We'll be safe to gather there for the trek south."

Stephen gazed up into a wall sconce burning pungent oil. "If we set that many people struggling over ice ridges across miles of ice, the stragglers will run out of daylight and become vulnerable. Daylight's only two hours long."

Albert sagged, looking exhausted. "I'm sending them."

"I'm the captain," Stephen said. "You won't send them."

"I can't begin to describe what we've fought through," Albert said softly. "We've faced worse than death and lost a lot of people. I've performed dozens and dozens of funerals for people who've gone mad and had to be put down like rabid dogs. So many. But go ahead. Order them to wait for spring. Let's see who they follow."

The group looked shocked, but Stephen held out his hand. "Let's continue this in the captain's quarters."

Albert looked at the hand, then stood without taking it, walking aft.

The small, formerly tidy cabin that Stephen once occupied was a jumble of blankets and coats and books. A hammock had been hung over the cot to handle the ship's current tilt. Albert lived here now, but Stephen was still captain and Albert's mind wasn't what it had been. These squids had got inside his head.

"You don't understand what's under us," Albert insisted as the door closed.

"Miles of dark water, and some whale-squids."

They glared at each other, all wind-burned cheeks and chapped skin. Stephen looked away first, and his eyes caught on a heavy book on the captain's table. It was open to a page with a rough map drawn in heavy lines. Hatter's Island. The text lay in neat columns, and though he could read Talian and Haisse, and he'd seen five or six other writing types, these symbols were new to him.

"Is this from the second sailing ship?" he said, running his fingers over the page.

"Yeah. It's a strange ship, with an oddly compartmented hold. Odd dimensions. I have a crate of stuff down below—clothes and utensils and some ink drawings that hung on the walls. A bunch of books. It's from a culture I've never encountered."

"Albert," Stephen said over his shoulder. "There's a logical explanation for this, you know it. And walking the passengers out after sitting here for months, with women and children and invalids, won't save them. Even if we got them to Maycomb. We need to steam out on coal. We need the ice to melt." He flipped a page gently. More indecipherable symbols written in a cramped hand. There was a rough drawing, scratching in angry lines, of a monster with a squid head that had a dozen arms along its armored body. The claws were overly exaggerated. Stephen frowned. "Whales swim in pods. Do these squids swim together under the ice? Or are they loners?"

"They always rise together, way out between Maycomb and Hatter's. I think it's very deep there. Then they swim in on the surface, breaking ice."

"Always on the surface?"

"Not always. They dive sometimes and breach suddenly. Especially when there's a sound they can follow."

"How many are there?"

"There are three; there used to be four. When we killed the little one," he laughed at his own description of it being little, "they attacked. Lucky us, they seem to be blind, relying on sound to hunt. They'd smash through the ice, then submerge and rise up again a short while later. There was nothing we could do but hang on and pray and stay silent. That went on for most of a day, but they never found us in all that broken ice. We were left intact, and the corpse of the little one floated about a quarter of a mile off."

"Floated?"

"They'd broken that much ice. The water refroze over the following days, and the ship tilted as the ice shifted." He tapped his boot lightly on the wooden deck. "Once the ice froze, we walked to the dead thing and fired up the triworks on the whaler."

Suddenly, the door swung in and a big man still in his outdoor coat leaned in. "The Queen M's going over," he said urgently but quietly.

"What?" Albert demanded.

"The ice must have cracked under her when the beast swam past."

"Dammit!" He looked at Stephen. "You brought them back on us."

They rushed across the grand salon, which was now empty, grabbing coats as they went. Outside, the deck was crowded, but they forced their way through to the rail.

Stephen could clearly hear the death-groans and snapping wood of the old whaler above the wind. "Yeah, she's going over." And she was fighting it all the way. Were the holds collapsing one by one? Couldn't she die in quiet dignity? He just made out her silhouette by starlight.

"They're coming!" someone called. "Due south."

People swarmed the harpoon guns and raised rifles.

"Quiet!" Albert called. Silence fell except for the wind and the agonized splintering of the *Queen Mandage*. Everyone watched and waited.

"The Queen M is a hundred yards off," Albert said softly, "so they'll miss us when they follow the sound. They'll circle on her a few times, though, and that's where we could take a hit."

Stephen's heart hammered as he gripped the nearby railing. Were these things really as big as the *Butterfall*? From the approaching sound, they weren't terribly fast, but they were massive. Breaking ice couldn't be easy, even for an animal their size.

Then the beast was upon them, sweeping across to starboard, pushing up a swell of water that splintered ice all around and shook the *Butterfall*. The ice-cracking stopped as the things submerged, and Stephen clung to the railing, listening. Then he heard the impact of something large and determined striking up into the wooden whaler from below. A moment later he heard a second splintering boom.

"That's two of them," he gasped as the *Queen Mandage* elevated her shrieking and cracking into an aria of collapse. He could just make out the bow and stern rising to the sky and broken masts being dragged across the ice by rotten ropes before everything slid into dark water.

"We'll be killed," Albert whispered.

"No one's dead yet," Stephen replied, heart still drumming, eyes straining to pierce the darkness. "They're coming around, like you said." A new sound of ice shattered to the south told him that the third beast was coming to join the pod.

The three swept back across the *Queen Mandage's* grave on the surface at an angle to the *Butterfall* and set the tilted steamship shaking violently again.

"Hang on," Stephen said.

Slowly, inexorably, as ice cracks joined and propagated and burrowed, the *Butterfall* moaned angrily and began to right herself. As the downside paddlewheel rose, it lifted a massive block of sea ice into the air, water pouring from its surface.

"Too much noise," Albert muttered, eyes stark.

Then they came across a third time, so close that Stephen could see the wash pouring off their immense backs. *God above, they're big*! He held on as the ship rode up and over the swell and heard stifled cries from passengers being tossed around inside.

The beasts circled once more, slightly farther away this time, and then headed south a little. The shattering-ice noise continued. Relieved laughter broke out across the deck. People let go of the railings, hugging each other.

Stephen stood, feeling like laughing himself. He elbowed Albert. "You did good."

"If you hadn't come, they never would have sunk the Queen M. They're not going to give up now, they know we're here somewhere."

"I was never *not* going to come, Albert. What, were you planning on sitting here for the next sixty years until you were the last survivor? The beasts would have gotten you eventually. Or starvation or cold. Now we have to deal with the situation at hand."

Stephen made his way to the bow through the crowd. Newly broken ice thumped against the hull with a soft, hollow echo as the wind whistled around the wires and smokestacks. Albert, Annie, and Randolph joined him. The beasts were circling slightly to starboard now.

"Look at that," Stephen said quietly.

The three beasts had arrived together along roughly the same line. Glistening under the brilliant starlight was an open swath of water, more than wide enough for the ship to steam through.

"They've made an open channel toward Maycomb," Annie marveled. "It's not straight and it may not be continuous, but this is the only chance we have until Spring."

Albert's eyes went wide. "No, no, we can't. They'll hear the beating paddles."

"This ship can steam at almost twenty miles an hour," Stephen reminded him, "even through broken ice, and we're faster than that if we give the engines everything we've got. We'll outrun them."

"They'll come at us from underneath!"

"Then we'll give them a reason to chase us on the surface," Randolph said.

"How?"

"Dynamite. A big explosion to the north. They'd go investigate, and we'll start the paddlewheels."

"You have dynamite?" Albert's voice verged on hysterical. "Because we don't."

"We brought two crates. Waterproof dynamite."

"Let's say this works. Let's say they go after the dynamite and then chase us; the open path won't reach all the way to Maycomb. What happens when we run out of water?"

"I timed it as they swam south," Stephen said. "Assuming we can steam as fast as they swim, we have ten minutes before we run out of water. And when they catch us, we'll fight."

"That's insane."

"You killed one."

"We got lucky! It surfaced next to us, and someone got it in the eye with a harpoon. It's the only place they're vulnerable." He looked away. "Three of our harpooners went insane from looking too close. We wore blindfolds when we butchered if for blubber."

"Well, we can't wait here while they search for us, you may not get so lucky twice." Stephen looked at the line of harpoons and their steam launchers along both sides of the ship. "Do you have explosive bolts?"

"Of course not, the barbs from the whaler are too old for that. We've modified the launchers with steam to give them more punch, but that's all."

"Then we'll tie dynamite to the shafts, up near the head. We can do some real damage that way. We'll line harpoons along the stern for when the beasts get close, and we'll make sure people don't look directly at them."

"You can't aim with your eyes closed."

"Look, Albert, if they're right behind us on the surface, following, they're sitting ducks. Aim with peripheral vision."

He shook his head angrily but said no more.

Stephen turned back to the open path of water stretching from the bow. A beast circled wide and came by the *Butterfall* to port, then circled back south again. Were they using any sort of strategy to search? His heart was beating fast. "When we start, we'll need navigators to guide us. Do these bowlamps have oil?"

"No," Albert snapped.

"Fill them. And we'll need flagmen on the bow to signal up to the pilothouse. And people with gaffer poles to push the bigger ice blocks out of the way."

"What happens if we hit an unbroken patch of ice?"

"The bow is reinforced and sharpened for icebreaking. Just in case, though, let's put carpenters inside the bow for emergency repairs."

"I'll lead the dynamite team to the north," Randolph said. "We'll light 'em up about a mile behind the ship, then we'll run for Hatter's Island. There'll be so much going on, the beasts won't hear our steps. And we'll rejoin you at the Maycomb camp."

Stephen hugged him hard. "Go fast, and don't do anything stupid."

Stephen and Albert visited the engine rooms, one for each paddlewheel. The boilers were already hot with monster oil, which Stephen had to admit smelled as nauseating as Albert had warned. Not just bad, it raised the hairs on his neck. They were only using the boilers for heat, so the steam pressure was low.

"We could use coal," he said to Albert. "We brought a sled full."

"The oil's more powerful. Stick with it for this suicidal run, then we'll switch back to coal at Maycomb Island." He looked at several barrels to the side of the boiler room. "I can't stand this stuff. It gives everyone nightmares."

Stephen nodded. "Raise the steam pressure slowly," he told the engine men. "When you hear the dynamite go off, that's only the start. As soon as we're sure the beasts have chased the dynamite, we'll ring the pilot's bell like mad."

He glanced up at the bell and saw that it had been wrapped heavily in cloth, and he tugged it off. "Once we start, give every bit of pressure you can to the rocker arms."

Back out on deck, Stephen and Albert passed among the crowds of passengers, softly ordering everyone back inside. Randolph waited for them at midship with four men. They each carried a bundle in a bag around their neck.

"We'll set the first batch about a mile back, and then a second batch closer to Hatter's Island as we run. Maybe a third. We'll distract them for as long as possible."

Stephen looked at each of them, though he could barely see who was who under all their layers. "Thank you, all. You'll give us a chance, and we're going to take every inch of it. Be safe out there."

The men climbed down the near sidewheel into a whaler rowboat and poled across the broken ice to the stable icesheet with what Stephen feared was too much noise. But then they disappeared into the darkness.

The breaking ice from the beasts continued to port.

Stephen hefted an axe and moved toward the portside paddlewheel—the downslope wheel that had been most deeply embedded in the ice. The ice still encased the paddles, and it had to be over three feet thick. There were more men waiting with sledgehammers. The wind dropped for a moment and he smelled foul oil-smoke from the stacks.

"The dynamite will be loud," he said quietly to the men around him and still saw several of them wince. No one talked on deck here, but he wasn't afraid of a whale-squid. They were beasts that could be killed. Big beasts, who could destroy ships, who were audibly still circling. As for the time-discrepancy and the appearing and disappearing ships—that was a hallucination brought on by the stress of the cold and darkness and the magnetic anomaly. "If these wheels aren't free of ice when the rocker arms engage, the whole thing will tear itself apart. When the dynamite goes off and the beasts head north, hit it with everything you've got."

He patted his pocket watch, feeling the shape of it, but didn't take it out. It ticked against his chest. "It'll take them about thirty minutes to get a mile away and set the dynamite."

Thirty minutes was a long time to wait and pace and listen to the sea monsters hunt. Stephen felt the cold in his bones as ice-rime formed like skin on the open water around them. He swung the axe back and forth to keep blood in his hands.

Then the dynamite finally went off with a clap that bounded across the ice. Everyone jumped and Stephen spun to look. It wasn't simultaneous, several explosions overlapped, and the boom rolled over the ship like thunder. Immediately, the beasts and their ice-breaking sped north past the *Butterfall*. Stephen hated being blind. He imagined great, dark squid bodies swimming.

"Break off the ice!" Stephen called, swinging his axe. "Quickly."

So they hacked and chopped while the team on the opposite side did the same, and in several minutes, the paddlewheels were clear.

Everyone straightened, waiting, hammers and axes held across their bodies. Oil-smoke poured up into the frigid air, whipped away by the wind. The ship rocked gently.

How would they know when the whale-squids reached Randolph's dynamite?

"Man the harpoons," he said softly to the gathered people, then hurried up the exterior stairs to the pilothouse where Albert waited. He'd opened the forward windows to hear better, and his hand was on the bellpull down to the engine room.

Stephen joined his old first mate and they stared out into the darkness together. Below, teams gathered at the harpoons. Out across the ice, Randolph and his dynamiters were hopefully clear of the first blast, heading for Hatter's Island, setting the second batch of dynamite.

"Pray you don't see one," Albert said under his breath.

"Okay." But Stephen actually wanted to see what had besieged the ship all these months. He'd seen the glossy, black back of one, but not the thing itself. Was the drawing in the strange book even close? That was a horror to tell your children about.

Stephen heard the second dynamite detonate with a rumble. "That'll pull them father off," he said. "Ring the bell!" He picked up a rifle from several by the wall and checked that it was loaded.

"Don't shoot unless they're right on us, and aim for the eyes." Albert shuddered.

He yanked the two bellpulls sharply over and over while Stephen raced down to the paddlewheels. The ship shuddered as the engines' speed increased and the rocker arms engaged. The giant wheels turned, shrieking against solidified axle grease. Stephen watched the paddles critically as they lifted from the water. A few were broken, but most had held. Teams smacked ice off them as they rose from the depths.

A third burst of noise and thunder rolled out on the ice-plane, this one from close to Hatter's Island. *Thank you, Randolph.*

Jumpy, Stephen joined the navigators and flagmen at the bow. The bowlamps were blazing, illuminating twenty feet or so of black water and bobbing ice. It was going to be horrible, navigating through this, especially while being chased.

He drew out his pocket watch. The second hand jumped around, but it seemed to be ticking true. There was nothing for it but to count to sixty and mark the minutes, because they had ten minutes of safety. He slipped it into his palm, inside his mitten, and began to count.

The paddlewheels were churning now, beating the sea and flinging saltwater across the deck. Lines of seafoam trailed as the sluggish *Butterfall* gained speed. *Come on!* The flagmen raised their white signal flags, pointing at two o'clock, and Albert turned the ship into the shattered lane of ice, hull booming and growling from impacts. Signal flags to midnight and Albert straightened her up; then to eleven o'clock. Navigators leaned forward over the bow rail, shouting at each other, trying to come to a consensus of the best way forward.

One minute gone.

They were truly in the lane now, sometimes wide, sometimes so narrow the wheels scraped the sides. Stephen could just make out the darkness of Hatter's Island on his right as they moved across it. Where were the beasts? They'd come at a diagonal from the last dynamite location, cutting the distance.

Thick ice caught a paddle with a terrible crack, and an empty slot came up on the next rotation of the wheel. Flags hard to nine o'clock for a jog, and then back to midnight.

Two minutes.

They struck an intact bridge of ice and the ship stuttered. There was shouting belowdecks. The paddlewheels thundered on and the nose of the *Butterfall* rose sharply before coming down on the ice, breaking it. Twice more, and then they were through into another open lane. Once again, they gained speed.

Four minutes. Where were the beasts?

More shouting belowdecks, barely heard over the sidewheels, but he had to trust that the carpenters had leaking seams well in hand. Flags to eleven and then one.

Six minutes.

He hurried to check on the stern harpoon crews. Annie was in charge, with about twenty people with rifles in between the harpooners.

"Can you see anything?" he yelled. He was surprised to see three of the whaler's big rowboats dragging behind. He'd forgotten about those.

"Nothing, and I can't hear anything over the paddles. They're going to come up on us suddenly." She looked spooked, but he knew she was calm in a crisis.

They were past Hatter's Island now, into the three-mile stretch between Hatter's and Maycomb where the wind really found its rhythm. The steamboat leaned to port against the gale.

Eight minutes. Signal flags whipped back and forth, and the ship steered to match.

Stephen hustled back to the pilothouse where the noise was worse, if anything. "Nine minutes," he yelled.

Albert watched the flagmen with intensity, twisting the wheel in response to their gestures. "They'll be on us."

"Annie's ready."

"No one's ready."

The ship rocked violently as they passed through an old ice-ridge and the wheels snaggled on it. A few more paddles snapped.

"Watch those!"

"I am, dammit, but that was too narrow to thread the needle!"

"Ten minutes. We're running out of lane," Stephen yelled. "Slow us. We've got to icebreak, and we can't do it at this speed."

"I am *not* slowing," Albert called back. "They'll come up under us if they can."

Stephen heard shouting and a crackle of rifle fire. He hurried out onto the pilothouse landing. "They're not coming up under us," he called back inside. "They're right behind us." The sound of breaking ice was unmistakable. Two of them were on their port and starboard sides in the heavy ice, bracketing their stern. One was in the water behind.

Steam launchers thumped, releasing harpoons. Two explosions followed seconds after; Annie had cut the fuses on the dynamite short.

He ran aft—seeing people reloading thick harpoons into the launchers as others bound dynamite to the heads. Someone lay on the deck, kicking and writhing.

"Did you get it?" he demanded of Annie.

"We got something," she said, voice shaking. "Something terrible. It dropped back when the dynamite went off, but I can't tell how wounded it is. You see that? The other two are on either side of us."

"They're herding us. What happened?" He pointed to the man who was down, thrashing. Someone was wrestling with him.

"He looked at it too closely."

Stephen felt a chill flush down his spine, colder than the howling wind, and a pistol shot went off. The writhing man fell limp and the wrestler stood.

"What did you do?" he yelled, grabbing the wrestler by the coat.

The man turned to face him, pistol half up, and then he lowered it. "It was a mercy," he called back. "You can't leave him like that. He'd be tearing his own eyes out in a few minutes or attacking us while we fight. It was a mercy." He holstered the pistol and then he and another man roughly dragged the dead man out of the way.

Shaking his head, Stephen returned to the stairs up to the pilothouse, and caught sight of the flagmen's white flags go straight down to six o'clock.

"Albert! Stop the engines. We'll rip hell out of the bow if we hit the ice at this speed. That's an order!"

"They're waiting for it. When we slow, they'll ram us from the sides."

"They'll have us when we hit the ice no matter what." Stephen looked at the harpooners, the sidewheels, and the black, undulating, glossy backs of the beasts poking up through shattering, scattering ice. "Stop the wheels. When we slow, they'll come in close to ram, and then when we hit the ice, they'll overshoot us. We can attack them then."

Albert looked like he was going to say something, then nodded, looking sick.

Stephen left the pilothouse and ran to the bow again, shouting for everyone to hang on. To prepare to shoot as the beasts passed. He didn't know what he was shouting. In the light of the bowlamps, he could see the end of the water coming where the beasts had first surfaced.

The wheels slowed and then stopped, dragging the ship. The *Butterfall* was slowing, but not enough, and the wind howled like a banshee. The beasts closed in.

"Hang on," he yelled, but his words were snatched away by the wind. His pocket watch ticked against his palm inside his mitten.

The hit, when it came, was terrible, driving the bow up onto the thick ice sheet. Stephen could feel wood crack through his boots and hear it over the wind. Chips and splinters flew. Hanging on, he jerked his head back to see where the beasts had got to just in time to witness the aft harpooners release directly into their armored sides on both port and starboard. One after another, the harpoons shot as the things passed. By the time they'd reached midships, the first sticks of dynamite went off in wallops of sound and force. Harpoons kept shooting all the way to the bow, and dynamite kept exploding.

Flashblind, blinking, Stephen had to believe that they'd done crippling damage. The two things were ahead of the bow now, thrashing and coiling, barbed tails whipping. Ice smashing everywhere. He yelled to the forward-most harpoons to shoot again if they had the range.

Suddenly, there was a crash from the stern and the bow heaved up off the ice and stayed there. Voices cried out. Screams.

Stephen spun to see a giant shape blotting out the stars, clambering onto the stern of the ship. Gunfire erupted, sporadic and then nearly continuous. He broke into a run down the tilted deck, bellowing at the harpoon crews to shoot. They couldn't swivel the launchers enough to shoot across the deck, and men were scrambling to pull up brackets to bodily move the entire mechanisms. It wouldn't work in time. The beast was pulling itself up.

Stephen grabbed his axe from beside the paddlewheel.

"Albert!" he shouted. A white face appeared in the pilothouse window. "Drive up the steam pressure. Do it!" The head disappeared.

Stephen strode around the main housing and had to force his legs to keep moving. There was wreckage and bodies strewn everywhere. Someone was throwing dynamite. Annie? And the thing towered over them.

The darkness of the beast was almost material, and the odor was overwhelming, hearkening back to an age of great monsters when humans were just cowering apes. Albert was right, the thing could not be described—Stephen's mind wouldn't latch onto words to describe the dizzying gulf of its enormous blasphemy. It was mountainous, vaguely anthropoid, with a corona of writhing tentacles around its head, and everyone was firing up into its open maw without effect. Where were the eyes?

Maybe it was the dim light, but Stephen held onto his faculties. He reached the last intact harpoon gun and stood on the steam hose, then chopped through it with the axe. A howling gout of superheated steam burst forth, billowing and clouding up. Stephen wrested it up under his armpit, using his coat to protect his side from burns.

"You don't like heat?" he cried, bringing the roaring steam flume up under the thing's belly.

It responded with a screaming shriek that was not made by lungs, and a clawed leg slammed down near where Stephen stood.

Someone else brought a steam hose up on the other side, while rifle fire crackled over the thing's wails. Feelers and tentacles were missing now from its head-corona, and it was backing up, leaving deep claw marks in the teak deck. Someone threw another stick of dynamite.

"Keep it going!"

They walked it back, step by step, across unspeakable slime and blood. Several people went down, thrashing, as their minds broke, but the rest remained resolute. And the thing, with one final, mournful cry, dropped off the stern and the *Butterfall's* bow fell back to the sea with a splash that staggered everyone.

Stephen stared into the aft darkness. The rails and harpoons were gone, and all the aft crew with them. He could barely comprehend what they'd done or how they'd done it. Then he returned to the bow.

"Where are they?" he demanded of a navigator, searching the quiet ice.

"Dropped out of sight," the woman said, arms crossed. "We hurt 'em bad. They slipped back down to whatever black, frozen hell they came from."

His next stop was to the carpenters under the bow. The freezing water was shin-deep in the compartment, but the damage wasn't as bad as Stephen had expected. Fresh boards had been nailed up over seams, and a lot of carpenters sported bandages, probably from when the ship had rammed the ice.

"Whatever you did to lift the bow out of the water, it worked wonders," the master carpenter said. "It gave us a chance to get ahead of the water."

"But can she still break ice?" Stephen asked. "I know she's damaged, but we have to keep moving for a little longer."

The master carpenter looked ill at the suggestion but nodded. "Go as slow as you can. We'll see that she stays together."

And so Stephen returned to the pilothouse at last. Albert stood on the outside landing and the beacon lantern was fully unshuttered to light the damage.

"We lost people," Albert said.

"We did. I think we lost Annie."

Albert shook his head in wonder, or maybe shock. "We beat them, didn't we?"

"They've gone down to lick their wounds in darkness, but we're not out of danger until we're out of this magnetic anomaly. I need you to steam into that new area the front two smashed open, and then very gently icebreak forward toward Maycomb until we're clear."

"How will we know?" His eyes were haunted.

"We're close to the edge. I'll stand on the bow with my pocket watch, and when it ticks true, then we'll know we're out."

And so he did.

The sun rose at last, as much as it ever did. The rescue party was there on the ice to greet them, having come out to the beacon lantern as the sun first began to lift over the horizon. Fifteen hundred survivors, plus or minus a hundred, gathered on the decks and on the ice, hardly daring to believe they were free.

Stephen went to greet Andack in front of his ice dwellers. They stood facing each other, holding each other's gaze.

"I told you not to go near Hatter's Island," Andack said eventually.

"You were right, but I had to. We fought off your Tolok god."

"That wasn't Tolok. You only faced its children. The ocean is ancient, full of memories and dreams from another age. Tolok sleeps in eternal darkness below."

Stephen winced at the thought, feeling deep exhaustion and grief. "Why didn't you tell me?"

"I didn't want to scare you."

THE CAMERA

I got to the hanger late, still furious I was even here, lugging my box camera and a case of fresh film plates in the back seat of my cabriole, and stopped at the top of the rise overlooking the valley.

I had to stop; it was just so impressive. For a moment I put away my anger and took in the scene. The Tiaga was already anchored tight to the servicing tracks on the ground and was being dragged slowly into the hanger, with a gaggle of news photographers close up under it. The *Saint Lucia* tug airship was tethered to the docking mast about a hundred feet above and looked dwarfed by the craft below.

My, my, the *Tiaga* was big. All dirigibles are, I guess, but I'd rarely cared to be this close to one before. As one of the great ships, the *Tiaga* stretched for over a thousand feet. The police crews and newsmen beneath it were smaller than ants.

I suddenly wanted a picture of it. I don't normally do out-doorsy stuff, or landscapes, or airships, but I was already late and would have preferred to be later, and it'd give the mortuary crews time to cart the bodies off. I hate bodies. Freezes me up to even think about them. And these bodies would be worse than normal. I can't even imagine.

I carefully set up my camera on its tripod and swung out the front and rear standards and bellows, careful of the aether-lenses inside. I had to hunt for my biggest brass lens to capture the breadth of the scene before me. I hardly ever use the wide lenses in my fashion practice, so it was still wrapped in its silk bag. The *Tiaga* was so large it had hardly moved much in all this time, so I carefully adjusted the focus, locked it down, and put a glass plate in. Since the owner, Thaddeus Greatmoore, was blackmailing me into this photographic excursion, I was going to expense every plate I took, whether it applied to the investigation or not.

Maybe I could make a little side money after this. Publish a pamphlet. I mean, how many dirigibles get lost over the Harrow Fields, and then return? Poor bastards on board probably didn't count it as lucky. I shivered. Very little ever comes back from the Harrow that one would welcome with open arms. I shivered again and tried once more to think of an excuse to get me out of this. Greatmoore had me good and had since our atelier days.

My only leverage would be the legendary quality of my photographs. The police always took bad pictures, and they were only ever really interested in the broad scene. The bodies and blood, and the damage. My camera was exceptional, magical even, and I lived and breathed tiny details in arranging my fashion models. Tiny details would be the thing to get Greatmoore out of this pickle. The newsmen were publicly excoriating his company with turgid and melodramatic headlines, but it would be the air marshals and the insurance men who could ruin him.

He needed me. He needed me to prove this was a straightforward accident and not negligence. And he needed me to prove that flying over the Harrow was still safe. All air traffic had ground to a halt since the *Tiaga* was lost, and his company was hemorrhaging money. Communication with the west had gotten difficult. Radiomen were trying to pick up the slack since the mail ships had been grounded, but there was only so much they could do... at least that's what I'd heard on the radio while driving over. I don't generally listen to the news, but this story was all anyone was talking about right now.
I folded my camera carefully back into its box, packed everything up, and made myself drive down the hill. The car bucked a bit, puffing steam, and I worried about throwing another rod. I hadn't brought my driver today, or any of my nice cars, because

no one could know I was here. I was dressed as a mechanic so the newsmen would pass me by, but that wouldn't hold if I showed up in a chauffeured Drapice. Not that I was a bad driver, I just didn't do it much anymore. I'd driven a considerable amount in my early days when I first started earning big money. I even learned how to work on the boiler and gears myself.

The *Tiaga* loomed higher and higher as my cabriole chuffed along, and when I passed into its shadow I hunkered down a bit. The temperature fell. It felt like leaving daylight and entering twilight. I still had a ways to go to get to the hanger parking lot.

There was a single, low office annex up against the hanger. A few newsmen waited by the door with a bunch of non-descript people who might have been family members of the deceased, but policemen kept everyone back. They waved me through when I showed them my temporary police papers. I hurried into the dingy airmen's lounge before any of the newsmen could recognize me through my coveralls.

The lounge wasn't much more than a few tables, a bar, a small toilet room, and the burn-reek of old cigarettes. There was a terrible chugging racket coming from the hanger that made it hard to think. Everyone was clustered at the back of the room, watching the *Tiaga's* progress through a pair of large windows into the hanger proper. The insurance people were at the left window and the airship people were clustered at the right with Greatmoore, keeping a bit of distance. The police chief and two air marshals with mammoth Haze guns over their shoulders stood between them.

Through the windows, I could see a full score of air marshals walking backward beneath the slow-moving *Tiaga* gondola. They all had their Haze guns pointed up. I stared at those heavy, iron hand-cannons, my unformed fears suddenly hardening into something much more defined.

I eased into Mr. Greatmoore's group and set my camera gently on a rickety table. Greatmoore stood with his thumbs in his waistcoat pockets, great belly straining the buttons of his vest. I counted three gold watch chains. Greatmoore had always lived to excess, even before he could afford it. Now the great industrialist could have anything he wanted.

I told myself sternly that he was the one in trouble today. Trouble he couldn't buy his way out of.

"You're late, Jack," Greatmoore grunted at me, not taking his eyes from the view.

He didn't need to be quiet. The steam crawlers out in the hanger that dragged the *Tiaga* thumped hard enough that I could feel them in my breastbone, and the air marshals shouted back and forth to one another as they covered the approach. The flight deck of the gondola was just reaching us, and I could see that most of its windows gaped open. The low air pressure at high altitudes had probably burst them outward. Hopefully it was air pressure, and not 'changed' passengers.

"I was getting a wide picture from the hill," I said.

Greatmoore grimaced. "The newsboys are getting plenty of pictures up there," he groused. "You can just pick up any daily paper tomorrow for a nice wide-angle view."

"The newsboys don't have cameras like this," I retorted.

He glanced at my camera and the ghost of a smile crossed his lips. "That's Edward's camera, isn't it?"

I refused to tremble before his implied threat. "Have the mortuary retrievers been on board yet?"

The police chief turned to me in annoyance. "Does it look like we've even gotten her settled yet?" he snarled. "The morticians will go on after my air marshals have cleared the ship. Not before. You'll wait with the rest."

I made myself not glare at him or retort because I was disguised as a mechanic. Stupid public servant. I could buy and sell him, if he only knew who I was. This could take hours! But then I saw the tight set of his jaw and how his eyes flicked back and forth between his air marshals out there and the broken windows and realized he was on edge. Frightened even.

I leaned back and looked over at the insurance men, and then looked around Greatmoore's crew. They all were. My throat tightened a little bit, and I vowed to never speak to Greatmoore again after this. This was the last 'job.' I should have told him no when he rang me up two days ago. I should have found the courage; except he could ruin me.

I comforted myself that he only rang me up every couple of years for some job that demanded my photographic talents.

The *Tiaga* had dominated the dailies for the past week, so that even I in my cloistered workshop was aware of it. The loss of a great ship over the Harrow Fields made headlines because dirigibles were guaranteed to be safe at higher altitudes. The prime minister always said so. The advertisements said so. Unfortunately for Greatmoore, a number of notable socialites had gone missing with his ship. The famous Harrow Hunter, Mr. Gregory Dallbot, and his Harrow-mapping team were among the missing, and the air marshal community was up in arms. Before the *Tiaga's* return, funerals had been planned without the benefit of bodies.

And then the ship suddenly reappeared over accessible land, clearly foundering. The dailies raced to one-up each other with dramatic headlines, both plausible ones like burst valves and ruptured hydrogen bags at high altitudes bringing the ship back down, or lurid ones about 'changed' people onboard flying their own way back out of the Harrow.

The tug-ship, *Saint Lucia*, on an emergency run had snagged the *Tiaga* out near Breslin before it could hit the ground or get blown into the city and brought it here. Away from population centers. According to the *Saint Lucia* crew, nothing living, human or 'changed,' had been seen through the widows. The air marshals clearly weren't taking chances.

Greatmoore pulled me aside a few minutes later. "It's going to be a long day, so pace yourself," he said, his eyes boring into me. "The mortuary crews will clear the bodies. I don't have to tell you to stay out of their way and step carefully. If you come across a body they missed or someone who hid in a closet, don't disturb them. Just call the mortuary director, Mrs. Hammels, and she'll set up a retrieval. Okay?"

I stared right back at him; my anger and fear surging. "This is the last one, Thaddeus," I said firmly. "This is the worst one."

"Which is why I need the best." He smiled a broad smile.

"I could die up there."

"Don't be so melodramatic. You're going to follow the morticians, the air marshals, even the police photographers, for God's sake."

"Last time." I poked a finger into his chest.

He smacked my hand away like I'd hoped, his smile dropping, and I knew that people rarely poked him anymore. "I told you it would be the last time, *if* this works out in my favor. Just make sure you photograph the valves and control sticks and gauges. Develop them right away. I'll get them to Mr. Creigh to analyze what the hell they were up to when they lost control of the ship. Take pictures of anything out of the ordinary. I'll have my structural men analyzing the internal struts and hydrogen bags, and my engineers review the engines." He nodded toward the gaggle of insurance men. "And they'll have their photographers and their engineers trying to prove it was our fault. The whole industry depends on it being my fault. They're desperate to make me a scapegoat so they can resume flights over the Harrow." He finished with a mutter, "Sometimes accidents just happen."

The air marshal chief grunted. "Could have been an accident, could have been crew error, could have been the Harrow itself, reaching up like the hand of the devil. Let the police determine the cause and stay out of our way."

The steam crawlers in the hanger suddenly went silent and it felt like my ears popped. Greatmoore and everyone turned. Air marshals fanned out as the *Tiaga* came to a gentle stop while the chief and his two lieutenants quickly went out through the door with a bang, letting in a cold gust of air that smelled like lubricating oil.

A police gang loudly pushed boarding stairs out to the belly dock, though the stairs were a mismatch since a ship of *Tiaga's* size would never normally have been boarded from the ground. As it was, the rolling stairs were about four feet too short, and the air marshals would have to hoist themselves up. Mortuary crews in their protective suits gathered. You didn't take chances with the Harrow.

Greatmoore was frowning, staring hard through the window.

"The ship's engineers might have moved the controls in an effort to get ahold of the ship once they knew they were in trouble," I said quietly to him. "Don't get your hopes up that this'll be cut and dried. Most likely it'll come back 'undetermined cause'."

He didn't respond for a long minute, though I could see his eyes tighten. He took a deep breath at last and said without looking at me, "I'll get copies of the police photographs. We can see where the bodies ended up. That might tell a story — whether it was quick or slow."

I turned back to the window, a pit in my stomach as air marshals in gasmasks climbed the stairs to unbolt the hatch. Haze guns were out and aimed at the hatch by the air marshals on the ground. My hands were clenched and I consciously relaxed them. I really didn't want to see the bodies. I'm intensely visual, and I knew they'd be stuck in my dreams for weeks. I didn't want to know what the Harrow had done to them.

I'd flown over the Harrow Fields twice, it's the only way to get to Drannislyn and the western cities now that it's cut the country in half, but I couldn't remember it. No one can. It does things to your memory. The Harrow mappers have to draw quickly in flight, and they never remember what they've drawn afterward. But what they drew, I've read, is enough to give any sane person nightmares.

The Harrow Hunters actually go into it wearing protective gear. They're famous. There are popular books written about them that I'll never read. They even managed to recapture the city of Tyffin and push the Harrow back last year, their one significant victory. No one wants to live in Tyffin now, but still... it's symbolic.

The hatch swung down, and the assault-lead shoved his head and Haze gun up through the opening. A moment later, he waved 'all clear' and climbed aboard. His companions cautiously followed one by one. The mortuary crew, in heavy canvas suits and full-head gasmasks, waited with stretchers and body bags. The police photographers had their cameras under their arms, and I noted that they looked battered and old. Not like my mythical beauty. They boarded after the last of the air marshals. Then the morticians.

The removal of bodies proceeded fairly rapidly, I guess, but it still seemed endless at the same time. Two morticians would stand at the top of the stairs, hands raised, and a stretcher, tightly wrapped in canvas, would descend. They would hustle down, and another pair would take their place. There were just so many bodies. Forty passengers and nearly thirty crew. I wondered where they were taking all the bodies, and then decided I didn't want to know. Curiosity only ever got me into trouble.

Funny thing was that though the belly hatch and stair were crawling with morticians, not a single air marshal had yet returned. I guess they had to check every nook and cranny, even up into the hull on the spiderweb of catwalks and platforms. Once I saw two men cross on an exposed walkway out to one of the mammoth engine cars on an outrigger.

I broke into a cold sweat, my heart thumping. How was I going to go out onto that? I was hyperventilating. I closed my eyes and forced my breathing to slow. It helped a bit.

I heard muttering around me and opened my eyes to see the police chief jogging down the stairs. A number of morticians followed behind him with no new bodies.

He banged through the door, pulling his heavy, rubber gasmask off with a hard yank. "You," he barked, pointing at me. "You're up. The bodies are off and I want to quarantine this thing before the end of the day." He looked at the insurance men. "You too."

Their photographer and a pair of mechanics separated from the group, looking just as frightened as I felt. As we moved forward, the chief stepped back, crossing his arms. "They all died of asphyxiation as far as we can tell, probably due to the altitude. Any blood seems incidental to them falling on edges and corners. My detectives are still on board. Don't get in their way. Don't touch anything."

Two men separated from Greatmoore's group and followed me. Probably his engineers. Greatmoore nodded to me.

I made my way through the door into the cool, diesel-scented air of the hanger and grabbed a gas mask from the police bin. It said 'Air Marshal' in yellow stencil on the side and was uncomfortably heavy. I hadn't worn one since the scare back at the atelier—what some would call an art enclave—when I was twenty-two. The insurance photographer and I shared a look, and then he hurried up the stairs after his team, his tripod balanced on his shoulder, the camera already screwed on. I followed, lugging a case of about twenty plates. You never know how many photographs you might need to take. Morticians continued to pass us heading down, hurrying to be clear of the derelict. More than one stared at me through their distorting gasmask lenses.

I carefully placed my camera and cases in the hold and wriggled myself up like a floundering guppy, fully aware of all the eyes watching me through the windows below. The mechanics and insurance photographer were already past the stacks of equipment and packaged food and were hurrying up an iron staircase to the main deck. I forced myself to go slow and document everything. I'd get Greatmoore out of this fix, but I had to do it properly.

It felt deathly quiet beyond my breathing through the gas mask as I set up my tripod and took my first photograph of the neatly stacked supplies and a mortician walking up the narrow path through them toward me. The flash was bright and left both of us shaking our heads and him cursing at me. The mortician shoved past me and dropped through the hatch, and I was alone. Why couldn't I hear any air marshals talking or moving above?

I felt like someone was watching, standing right beside me, following behind. My nerves, tense after the last two hours of waiting, were getting the best of me, right? Maybe I should move a little faster, even as I took careful pictures.

I hurried forward to the stairs, lingering for a moment to photograph the grand, carpeted entrance behind the stairs where guests would normally have boarded in comfort. The filigree along the molding was gilded and lovely; but the oppressive feeling of someone standing beside me was too much to linger there for long.

I hauled the equipment up to the main deck where air marshals in groups were finishing their sweep or were talking intently to each other. Thick carpeting ate all sounds of footsteps, so that explained the sepulchral silence. Behind me stretched a narrow hall to the sleeping cabins, and forward was the wide lounge/ dining room. An air marshal stopped me, as he was about to start up the stairs to the crew level above. His great, bristly moustache brushed the glass of his gasmask.

"When you get to the Control Room," he called, "don't mind the blood. Looks like they toppled over at their posts."

"They warned me," I called back. "So it was a quick death?" Maybe Greatmoore would be lucky, and the levers and valves would all be in their original positions.

"I doubt it," the man said. "Most of the passengers were at the front observation lounge, so there was time to gather. There are still a bunch of detectives up there, so you might check engineering first." He pointed down the corridor between the sleeping cabins.

I nodded and gathered my nerve. There was nothing here, really. The air marshals had been all through it. The morticians had been here by the dozen. Except there *was* something here and it had me jumping at every noise. Being unable to see out of my peripheral vision with the gas mask on made it worse.

I walked down the plush, maroon carpet, moving as quickly as possible while remaining calm and in control because I didn't want to bang my camera on anything. The doors of the sleeping cabins all hung eerily open, revealing bits of abandoned personal lives, but I saw no other living person. The air marshals had finished their sweep down at this end.

I was also alone in the engineering car, which sat at the far back of the ship and below the stern cabins. It was claustrophobically tight, with windows on either side that looked out on the ship's engines. I had a tough time mounting my tripod far enough back from the controls, but I took several photographs of gauges, levers, and the banks of hydrogen valves, as well as the broader room. The telephone handset to the forward Control Room hung by its wires and I had a sudden urge to put it to my ear to see if anyone was there. I turned cold at the thought of it touching my skin and took a photograph of it instead.

It's funny how my mind started playing tricks on me. I swear half a dozen times I thought an air marshal was behind me, moving about, looking at dials and gauges, but no one was ever there when I turned. Maybe heading forward was a good idea, even if I got in the way of detectives.

I hustled up the steps to the central corridor where the cabin doors all stood closed now, and lugged my equipment toward the main, forward lounge. This was where the passengers would have dined and passed the time. The *Tiaga* was large enough that it probably had a mezzanine and promenades that wrapped around the outside of the cabins, against the gondola's windows.

I stopped in the door. The detectives had moved on, because there were only a few people in the airy, ornate room. Three young air marshals in gas masks scooped up personal possessions from the floor and tossed them into canvas bags. The insurance photographer was just hefting his camera. He met my eyes quickly, nervously. He felt it too. The silence was heavy. He crossed the dance floor toward the forward control room, leaving me with the three air marshals.

I set down my tripod, wanting a picture of this, though it technically wasn't part of Greatmoore's requested photographs. I told myself it was to compare them with the police photographs later. See what had been moved by the air marshals and morticians. Tables and chairs lay scattered everywhere, but some might have been righted or shifted aside. Cushioned benches along the outer walls were swollen with rainwater. Most of the slanted windows that followed the curve of the gondola's walls had shattered outward, leaving no glass behind. Books had tumbled from bookshelves.

They'd been through one hell of a storm. Before or after?

I was glad the bodies were gone. The atmosphere of catastrophe was harsh enough and the feeling of being stalked that had started in the storage hold below had not abated a whit. If anything, it grew worse.

"Find anything interesting?" I called to the air marshals, just to break the silence.

They jerked up as if I'd kicked them, then waved me off in obvious relief. "Make a little noise when you come in, would you?" one called. "We're on edge."

"I'm not going to sleep for a week," said another.

I nodded and clamped my camera down to the tripod so I could take a photograph to starboard, then to port.

Dragging my gear forward once more, following the insurance photographer, I found my shoes squelching on wet carpeting. I passed a white piano, the veneer swollen and buckled. Pain suddenly shot up my calf like an electric shock and I jumped, fearing there was an exposed electric line somewhere in the wet carpet. I hurried on to the forward door of the control car. Feeling all nerves, I made myself stop and take another picture of the lounge, facing sternward. The three air marshals were throwing things indiscriminately into their bags, moving fast. I'd vowed never to break in the face of fear again after the atelier burned when I was twenty-two.

I didn't see acquiescing to Greatmoore as giving in to fear, blackmail was the cost of doing business, but I knew I would never bow before him again.

Sliding my latest photographic plate into my case, I turned to see the insurance photographer lifting a lever in the far-forward steering room. Maybe if I hadn't stopped to take that picture he would have heard me coming, but I caught him red-handed and he knew it.

"What are you doing?" I demanded, striding forward, my tripod and camera forgotten. I was absolutely furious. If the insurance guys were changing things, then they were really out to screw Greatmoore, and I'd never get my life back. "What are you doing?" I demanded again, grabbing him by the lapels of his coat and shoving him back. I could see his wide eyes through his gas mask.

"Nothing!" he yelled. "I wasn't doing nothing."

"You moved a lever!" I was bellowing now, shaking him. He crumpled, knees buckling, and I let him fall. "I'm going to take a picture of this room and compare it to the police photographs from earlier. Any control levers or valve handles that've been moved, and I'm calling an inquest on you."

"No, don't," he begged. "They told me too. They told me to get ahead of you and change things. They said the police wouldn't focus much on the levers."

"Idiot." I stood, lowering my hands to my sides. "You think the police didn't capture the controls when they were photographing bodies? Don't touch another thing. In fact, get off this ship."

"But I'm not done," he cried.

He scrambled to his knees beside his tripod, which was still facing forward toward the prow. He looked alone and terrified. I raised my fists again, trying my best to be imposing like I did with difficult models. "Give me the plate you just took."

"What?"

"Give me the plate you just took, and the two before that. Then get off this ship."

He stood slowly, then reluctantly pulled three plates from his case, handing them over.

"These better be the right ones, or I'll call for an inquiry," I said. I glanced down at the edges of the plates. They were Balder plates. Inexpensive pre-mades. Not bad quality, probably better than the police ones, but nothing compared to my homemade ones. I prided myself on making silver-nitrate gelatin plates better than the best commercial ones available.

"I can't leave," he said, muffled through the mask. "I have to take the pictures for the claim."

"Then they can send someone else up!" I shouted right in his face and pointed back toward the lounge. "Get off."

At last he scrambled, grabbing up his tripod, camera still attached, snatching up his photographic plate bag, and hurrying away. I stood and breathed slowly several times, air whistling through the filters on my gas mask. My temper sometimes got the better of me, but this was unacceptable. This was criminal. I hoped the police actually had captured the steering car in their pictures, but he might be right, and the police didn't show a single lever. They hired the worst photographers sometimes and used the cheapest equipment.

Then I caught sight of the blood and froze again, my anger melting away. It was everywhere in the steering car. There were a great many sharp corners and edged levers in here, and the dozen or so officers and crew seemed to have fallen on them with expert precision. There was a dried puddle of it beneath the port console. Only one window had blown out up here, though, so water damage was minimal.

Bringing my camera forward, I took several pictures of the equipment, then one of the adjacent navigation room with its maps laid out on the table.

I planned to take a picture of the radio console and its settings when I noticed a ladder and a ceiling hatch yawning open into darkness. I stared up for a long time, listening, wondering who had gone up there, and even turned around quickly once thinking someone had entered the navigation room with me. Then breathing slowly, I climbed the ladder with my camera and stuck my head through.

To say that the interior of the dirigible's hull was immense is not to do it justice. I was alone and insignificant in a vast space that wanted nothing more than to eat me. I felt like I could fall up into it. Distant tension wires *tang*ed softly as they shifted, and a vast hydrogen bag, one of many such lift-cells, groaned slowly as the ship swayed. The air was cold.

I saw no other people, either on catwalks or high service platforms, but frankly there could have been two dozen air marshals up there and I wouldn't see them.

I didn't like the cold feel of it either, which felt more like an oily indifference than a malevolence. I took one picture only, flash held aloft. Maybe it was my imagination, but when the flash flared the surrounding steel and wood to sharp relief, the groaning of the girders and gasbags increased and the feeling of being watched intensified. I dropped back down to the navigation room and pulled the hatch closed against the vast darkness.

I was done. I had to get out of here.

The nape of my neck was crawling as I slid that last plate into my case and folded up my tripod. The sound of my breath through the gas mask, the increased groaning of the ship, the conviction that someone was peering over my shoulder grew to be too much. Like an amateur, I didn't even unclamp the camera from off the tripod top but threw the whole thing over my shoulder and bolted out to the lounge.

The three air marshals were gone, and I was alone.

I crossed the dance floor at a run, leaping down the iron stairs to the hold and its bright exit hatch.

I laughed with utter relief as I reached the opening, as if I'd escaped something suffocating, and dropped down onto the stairs. There were a few air marshals standing below me and I waved joyously. They didn't wave back, and several looked startled. Haze guns swung around and trained on me, and my waving hand sank slowly to my side. Looking around, I saw that the owners and the insurance men no longer stood at the windows.

Clomping down the stairs now, mocking my own timidity, I yanked the gas mask off my head. "Well boys, that was an experience," I called.

Three advanced on the bottom of the stairs, Haze guns still up, and another half-dozen held back, keeping wider guard.

"What?" I said, noticing that those who held back wore blue-quartz goggles.

"Who're you?" barked the lead air marshal.

"I'm the cameraman for Mr. Greatmoore. Why? What's happened?"

"The clearing sirens were blown hours ago. Where were you when we ran the sweep?"

"Hours ago? What are you talking about? I was in there half an hour at the most. Did you bother to check steering? I'm not hard to miss, what with the tripod and all." My footsteps slowed as they didn't move or laugh at my joke. "Mind raising those barrels?" I asked.

"Let's see some identification."

I fumbled for my wallet, in my confusion forgetting that I was wearing a mechanic's jumpsuit instead of my normal suitcoat. As he inspected my identification and his companions with specialty goggles watched the open hatch, I looked around. The sun was low in the sky.

"That's not possible," I said, stunned. I felt hot, and the nape of my neck began tingling again. I looked over my shoulder. "Mind if I step into the airman's lounge?" I said.

"C'mon!" He grabbed my upper arm and pulled me along, and though I normally would have shoved him off and told him where to go, I found myself following along meekly, my tripod still over one shoulder and my case of plates banging against my hip. He took me into and then through the lounge to the parking lot where a large tent had been erected.

"Chief!" he yelled. Several air marshals appeared in the door of the tent, followed by the imposing figure of the air marshal chief shoving wide the tent flap. "He came off the ship. Says he's only been in for half an hour."

The chief sharply beckoned me in.

"What is this?" I tried to demand, but it came out weakly. "What's going on?"

"That ship's messed with everyone's minds, is what's happened," he grunted, turning back into the tent.

I followed him into noise and electric lights and a big, wireless aerial set-up in the center of the tent where police radiomen were chattering on microphones. There were reporters hanging about but the chief pointed at them immediately as they began to rush forward. "Sit! Down!" He turned to me. "Would you like a cup of coffee, Mr. Photographer? No cream to be had here, so you'll have it black and strong as turpentine, as God intended."

"My name's Jack, and that would be lovely," I said, eyes darting, having trouble putting thoughts together. There were a lot of people gathered in the tent, and not all of them had been here earlier. The reporters eyed me hungrily. I set my case on a table and tossed the police gas mask beside it, noticing for the first time that it looked burnt and curled at the edges. As the chief came back with a tin cup of coffee, I began to carefully unbolt my camera from the tripod and wrap the brass lens.

"You've been gone for six hours," the chief stated bluntly. "Most of my men got out after the first walk-through, but ten didn't come back with us. We searched and lost five more, and I sounded the evacuate claxon. Now seven of the missing have trickled back out with gaps in their memories and no concept of where the time's gone. You make eight."

"The Harrow?" I said horrified, thinking about the Harrow mappers who had to draw quickly while in transit because they couldn't remember anything afterward.

He nodded. "A bit of the Harrow seems to have come back inside that ship, though how much is a dicey question. We're going to tow it out again and release it into the poisoned lands, but I want my people back first. Harrow Hunters are coming. Belchick and Shadeki should be here by tonight with their heavy, protective gear."

Even I knew Andrea Belchick and Roderick Shadeki from the dailies. "It's that bad?"

"I'm not taking the chance. Tell me what you saw and where you went."

"I didn't see much at all," I kept my voice calmer than I expected I would. "Certainly not enough to warrant six hours. I took photographs in the Lounge, the Control Car, and the Engineering Car. That's it."

"Did you go up inside the hull? Did you climb up to the transverse catwalk and the crew quarters?"

"No. I might have if the ship was more inviting, but I felt like someone was following me at every turn." I shivered.

"*Everyone* felt that. Something's in there, and I've got men stationed with deep-sight goggles below the hatch to make damn sure it doesn't come out."

I stared at him silently as my heart drummed, aware the reporters were trying to listen over the chatter of the radiomen. "I didn't go up," I said when I found my voice again. "I only stuck my head up through the hatch in the Navigation Room, and then only for a minute."

"And that was enough. Everyone who's disappeared or lost time was up inside the hull."

I finished boxing up my camera with numb hands when I noticed a small stack of police photographs sitting on a table to the side. "You developed them already?" I asked.

He pointed to a back corner where a smaller tent had been set up within the tent. "Mobile darkroom. We were trying to figure out where everyone was and who was missing. One of my photographers came back, but not the other. This guy was mostly taking pictures of the bodies on the main deck. My other photographer went up into the hull to the crew quarters."

"May I look?"

He waved his hand. "Go ahead, but they're useless. Almost too blurry to figure out who's who. I fired the man immediately."

"Mr. Greatmoore will want copies anyway for his investigation."

"Then Mr. Greatmoore can request them himself, can't he?" the chief snapped. "He was the first to flee when it became clear people were missing. Him and all the airship executives. Cowards."

"Did the insurance photographer make it out?" Just thinking about him tampering with the levers got me angry again. "He should have come out early."

"I only have a roster of my people. Your people and the insurance people came and went without telling me, so they may all be down safely, or they may still be up inside." He picked up my case of plates and pressed it to my chest. "Develop these. I need to see if you photographed anything useful."

"I didn't take any pictures of your people; except those three young air marshals you left in the lounge to collect people's possessions."

He frowned. "I didn't ask anyone to pick up possessions. We weren't planning to empty the ship until our initial investigation was settled. That's someone else's jurisdiction."

"They were there, and they were gathering people's things. I saw them."

He looked down, frowning, his face growing dark. "Damn it all." He leaned close. "Bring me any photographs of them boys, and don't let on to anyone else that they exist, right? Bring me the negatives too. Everything. If I see so much as a hint of this in the dailies, I'll hold you responsible."

He didn't move his great, craggy face from mine, but I squared up against him and ignored the onion stink on his breath. "No need for threats. I'll get you your photographs, but I'm not developing them in that darkroom over there. That's the way to slop a negative. Let me go back to my studio and get them developed properly, and I'll bring them to the station tomorrow. I swear, I didn't take any pictures of your people other than those three, so there's nothing to develop and show you."

In truth, while I do take great pride in my work, I probably could have developed them in the mobile dark room. But I was thinking about Greatmoore and the blackmail and thinking I wanted to get away from this hanger as quick as humanly possible.

"Tomorrow," he said, still in my face. "Tomorrow morning. Telephone the station first, because we may still be out here."

With that he left the tent, heading in the direction of the hanger. I stared after him. So Greatmoore had run away? Idiot. Running away in front of reporters would only make it worse for him in the dailies. Public opinion was not in his favor, and I doubted any photograph of mine would change that. The competing airship companies were working to prove it was ship failure or crew error and not something endemic to the Harrow.

Several of the reporters sidled up to me as soon as the chief slipped through the tent door. "What's your name?"

I grimaced, not wanting my full name out there. "Jack," I said, running my fingers up through my hair, pushing it back where the gasmask had mashed it down.

"Hell of thing, isn't it? That ship? Must have been terrifying."

"Terrifying?" I knew their questions would try to shape a narrative, but I decided to shape a different one. Not that I wanted to do Greatmoore any cheap favors, but anything I could do to help him would loosen the grip he had on me. "Not, it wasn't that frightening at all. Empty, mostly. Your brain gets the better of you in there."

"But you were gone for six hours, man! What did you see?"

I pushed past them. "The morticians had the bodies off by the time I got on, so I didn't see anything." I'd been gone six hours. I couldn't fathom that number. Where had I gone?

"Hey, you lot!" bellowed the chief from the door on the far side of the tent. "Don't bother him." He glared until they backed off, then went for another cup of harsh coffee.

I nodded uncomfortably to the frustrated reporters and made my way around the radiomen to the police photographs. There were more than a dozen, and they were as bad as the chief had implied. Worse, maybe. The broad photograph of the lounge showed thirty or forty well-dressed, blurry bodies lying tangled and tumbled near the starboard window and the waterlogged piano. Several air marshals in gas masks stood nearby. Odd thing was that they were fairly sharp and clear. Maybe the photographer had his focal length off or something?

I stared closer. Something was really wrong with his camera. Probably a cheap department issue, or maybe his nerves had gotten the best of him, and he'd rushed. Too bad for the chief. There was a dark smudge off to the side that looked like a big dog but was probably some air marshal who had moved as the shutter opened. There were several mottled, diagonal lines across the whole photograph.

There were a number of pictures of the pile of bodies, closer but still blurry, that showed faces frozen in horror. You could make them out, though they were awful. One had been labeled in ink right on the picture with the name 'Gregory Dallbot'. The Harrow Hunter. He looked like he had an enlarged head.

There were pictures of the forward control car where the officers had not just fallen, but in some cases impaled themselves on levers and rods. Engineering looked calmer, with blurry men curled up on the floor. There were several photographs of people laying stretched out on the floors of their cabins as if they were carefully positioned that way.

I set the pictures down, rubbing my eyes, a headache growing. The police photographs were bad, Greatmoore was gone, a Harrow-tainted airship was looming over us all, and I'd lost six hours. I couldn't handle this all at once, so I stowed my equipment in my cabriole and left. I accelerated up the hill, kicking up dust, trying to escape those blurry photographs of frightened people clumped around a piano.

Wind whipped in my face, and I couldn't breathe properly. I couldn't see with the sun balanced on the horizon, and I nearly careened into a ditch several times. How had I lost six hours? I'd only stuck my head up through the hatch for a few seconds — long enough to take a picture. I had the picture somewhere in my case. A great picture of empty nothing, right? I got an uneasy feeling. What if I'd taken a picture of *something*?

Logic reasserted itself and I put on sunglasses before I killed myself. The sky on the horizon glowed in brilliant blues and greens, a sure sign that the western arm of the Harrow was stirred up. I was old enough to remember as a child watching the sunsets of pink and rose and gold, but that was before the Harrow stretched so far south.

Back home an hour later, dusk settling over the neighborhoods like a raven's wing, servants helped me out of the car and rolled it into the garage. They quickly got a fire roaring and brought out dinner, not asking any questions. I couldn't eat much, though. My eyes were drawn to the case of photographic plates standing just inside the foyer where I'd uncharacteristically dropped them.

I wanted them gone; I wanted this whole business done. I'd develop them right away and get them to Greatmoore and the chief. Might as well get it over with. I wasn't going to sleep anyway.

I hefted the case, leaving a plate full of food but taking my carafe of whiskey, and went down to my darkroom behind the studio at the back of the house.

I brought out the insurance photographer's plates first, because they were wedged in the front of my case. My headache was no better, throbbing behind my tired eyes, so I was generous in my pour of whiskey. The things I'd seen and experienced today? I'd encountered a bit of the Harrow. I might be infected now. My heart began to pound hard, and panic verged as I methodically fixed the negatives and inked the prints. The chief had let me go without protest, but how did he know I was safe? Was anyone? There was no way to be sure except to wait a few days. Even then...

I hung the pictures up to dry, studying them in the ruddy light. Two were taken in the Steering Car and were reasonably clear. Good. I'd be able to tell what levers he'd moved by comparing them to my photographs taken later. His third photograph was from the lounge before I got there, showing the starboard side with the piano and capturing one of the air marshals gathering possessions. It seemed a little blurry in the dim light. Mottled even, with more of those blurry, diagonal lines. Probably a bad plate.

I stepped out of the darkroom for a break and to refill my tumbler of whiskey, then touched my toes twice to try and release the tension gripping my shoulders. The sun had set behind the Harrow and the studio windows were dark, but my servants had lit a few electric lamps that I'd recently installed. They were brighter than the old gas-lamps, harsher perhaps, and I didn't normally like them. But now I appreciated their stark glare in my gloomy mood.

My memories of this long day were already receding like the tide, though the fear remained. Throwing back my whiskey and refilling it again, I returned with the tumbler to my plates and the task at hand. It seems I'd taken thirteen photographs, a great many for me.

The first was the morning's wide-shot of the Tiaga from outside on the hill. It showed excellent detail in the sun. I'd completely forgotten I'd taken it. I had, hadn't I? I'd been late to the gathering. True to form, my camera had produced a stunning work of art. Too bad no one would want to buy a print of the crippled *Tiaga*.

The next one was from the *Tiaga's* hold. I'd been straddling the open hatch, and some nameless mortician had been walking toward me in a protective suit and gas mask. The flash had burned dark streamers around him in an unfortunate halo. I suppose it looked interesting as an artistic effect, but I always strove to avoid gimmicks. The next one, of the empty and ornate loading room, was properly crisp and of my usual quality. Good. It meant there was nothing wrong with my camera. I knocked back my whiskey yet again, my tongue feeling numb.

I guess the three photographs in Engineering were passable. I could clearly see the levers and valves and the numbers on the gauges, but everything showed a faint shimmer of blur and there were the same mottling problems as the insurance photographer's. I returned to his lounge picture. Yes, very similar in faint diagonal lines.

Maybe it wasn't the quality of his plate! Maybe some effect of the Harrow had contaminated the silver nitrate.

What had we all been exposed to in there? What did the Harrow do to you? No one really knew, though scientists had cut up enough unfortunate souls who'd been caught in it. Harrow Hunters said that there were still people trapped there, but they were impossible to communicate with.

So with already fraught nerves, I nearly dropped the first print I developed of the lounge. It showed all of the piled bodies. How? They were sprawled in blurry, familiar contours around the piano. But that wasn't possible! This must be the poor-quality police photograph from before. That was the only explanation. The chief had slipped it into my case! The nerve of him, having a joke at my expense. I'd drive right over to the station in the morning and give him a piece of my mind.

But as I hung it up to dry, I knew it wasn't. I saw two of the three air marshals gathering possessions just off to the side. And while the bodies of the deceased were all hopelessly blurred, the two men were my camera's usual, crisp quality.

Hadn't I felt an electric jolt up my leg while stepping right into the midst of all those blurred corpses?

I fixed the second of my two lounge photographs and made the print, and this one I dropped. I had to snatch it back up from the floor before it got ruined.

Next to the three air marshals stood a lanky dog as big as an Irish wolfhound and black as night. It stared directly into my camera with half-lidded eyes. I'd seen a blurred, dog-shape in those police photographs too. This was real. It had been in there with us.

My hands shook as I emptied my whiskey tumbler yet again and stumbled back out of the dark room. My camera still lay nestled in its case by the front door, and I went to it and looked down at the worn leather. How was it capturing these things? Was it really a magical camera, as Edward had always claimed before the fire at the atelier? People had revered his photographs and compositions back then.

The camera was his masterpiece, an accidental invention made from bits of aether and etherea when we were just sixteen. Oh how he'd lorded it over us. It was going to take him to new, artistic heights.

"Will there be anything else, sir?" my manservant asked from an alcove, and I nearly jumped out of my shoes.

"Dembley! You frightened me half to death." I looked down at my empty glass. I was in no shape to drive. "Yes, yes there is something. We'll need to get to Thaddeus Greatmoore's house tonight. Get the car started in about half an hour."

I returned to the darkroom with slow steps, I'd only been delaying the inevitable, and I knew it. I needed to develop the final photograph. I needed to know what I'd seen inside the hull.

Harrow mappers never remember what they've drawn during flights.

So I pulled out the final exposed plate from my case and began to bathe it as the chemicals unexpectedly turned black. My fingers tingled, but there was no stopping this. I had to see.

The developed photo, which I carefully hung up to dry, did not show the vast, open interior of the dirigible that I remembered. I couldn't tell what it showed at first, just a miasma of shapes and blotched lines, until I brought my eyes close. Panicked, I slapped on the bright electric light overhead and stood panting, my hand on my throat, imagining that stalking presence from the ship was hovering over me now. My skin crawled.

I ran and fetched a magnifying glass and brought my eye close to the photograph again. The faint shapes leapt out under the lens, and I witnessed the sharp, tiny images of thousands upon thousands of people. Souls in torment. The damned. I could see their pleading eyes and the dark gashes of their howling mouths. Stumbling back, my arm with the magnifying glass sinking to my side, I also recognized that the blurred lines running diagonally across the photograph as the faint outlines of fingers and a hand clamped over the camera's lens. The images of trapped people were caught up in the whorls of the hand's skin.

I fled as fast as I could, heading for my telephone alcove off of the front hall, and rang the air marshal's station. It took three tries and two transfers, but I raised the radiomen in the tent at the *Tiaga's* hanger. Through them I got the chief.

"What the devil is this?" he demanded, his voice crackly over the miles. "I've got the Harrow Hunters here, and we're suiting up to go back in. I'm still missing a bunch of men."

"Chief! That thing isn't just tainted with the Harrow!" I was shouting so he could hear me. "I've developed my photographs. That ship *is* the Harrow. It's all there — inside. Maybe it's an arm of the Harrow, or a seed, but it's the real thing. The damned are all over the inside the hull by the thousands. You've got to get it back in the air and away from your people because it's boiling, I tell you, and it's going to boil over!"

"Damn," was all he said, then after a pause, "Right. I know what to do. You bring those photographs over round the station first thing in the morning, you hear me? I want to see what you saw."

Then he hung up and I gently set the earpiece back into place. I looked up to see several servants and my driver clustered tight in the hall looking terrified.

"Pray to God he listens to me," I said quietly to them. "Pray for us all."

"But what if the Harrow breaks out in Denton?" shrieked my head cook, a robust woman of advanced years.

"It's not just the chief working the derelict," I replied, taking her hand. "Half of the air corps is there, and the Harrow Hunters." I nodded to my driver. "But we'd better play it safe. Rouse everyone, children too, and take them west to Bratton. Spend a day or two over there, and if there's been no word of an outbreak, head on back."

"What about you, sir?"

"I'm heading to Greatmoore's. Leave me the cabriole."

We argued, but he didn't really want to stay with me in the area, so I found myself alone on the dark road, drunk as can be, on the way to Greatmoore's house about twenty minutes out into the knolls. I took my magical camera, Edward's magical camera, which had captured so much.

I was surprised not to crash on the way, and equally surprised when Greatmoore opened the door himself at my second knock. He wore his rumpled clothes from the day and was clearly as drunk as I was, because he embraced me as soon as he saw me.

"Jack."

"Thaddeus." I hugged him tightly back.

"I'm sorry I sent you up into that thing. I thought I'd sent you to your death when you didn't come back out."

"You don't know the half of it."

And so I told him as we sat over glasses of port in his private study, and he looked more and more shaken as he flipped through the photographs.

"The Harrow itself," he said, shaking his head. "Here at last. An ingenious way of getting behind our defenses, eh? Just like the Trojan Horse."

"The Harrow Hunters will handle it, I'm sure."

"Either way, we can't fly over it anymore. God help those people who died on board — they'll have to burn the bodies." He threw up his hands and sagged back into his chair. "That's it, then. It's over, no matter how much my competitors or the insurance men say that it was my fault and not the Harrow, the chief will tell the truth. The age of airships is done."

Greatmoore's entire fortune, his life's work, was built on dirigibles, so I knew he was speaking as much of himself as of the industry.

"No more than the ruins of anything else," I said, and pushed the camera across the desk to him. "Take it. Bring it to the police if you want, I won't deny my part in it."

His lip rose in a quick sneer that faded. "That's your livelihood, Jack. The source of all your stunning photographs. The source of your fame."

"Edward's fame. I killed him for it."

He stared at the closed case. There was no heat in his gaze, or any emotion at all. "You've been too squeamish to look at a dead body since, haven't you? Guilt is heavy."

"Even if I could, you wouldn't let me forget."

"He was a genius, wasn't he?"

"He would say that he was the best of us. You think he knew it could photograph the Harrow?"

"Knowing him, that was probably its original purpose, until he found out how beautifully it could photograph flowers and people and other mundane chaff." Greatmoore abruptly slid the camera back toward me. "Use it for its purpose. I won't blackmail you again, but you've got to promise to fulfill Edward's vision. Investigate the Harrow. Figure it out. Push it back, for all of us."

I reached out my hand. "If you promise to invest in Harrow-armor for the airships. Keep the flights alive."

Instead of taking my hand, he came around the desk and embraced me again, tears streaming down his face. Then he showed me out without saying another word and I drunkenly turned the cabriole and started off down his drive toward the main road.

It was about fifteen minutes later that a fireball blossomed very high in the sky, in roughly the direction of the *Tiaga*. I jerked the car to a stop and climbed out, staring up at the heavens. A boom like thunder swept across me as the flames glowed in vibrant blues and greens before collapsing into reds and raining toward earth. I watched the debris fall until the flames faded back into darkness, wondering if we'd been fast enough.

Had Edward really intended his camera for the Harrow?

Despite Greatmoore's assertions, I had always thought of Edward as a hopeless romantic when he wasn't being an arrogant prick. The Harrow was too much reality for him. I firmly believed his invention was only ever intended to reveal the beauty within the mundane, not pierce the veil of evil. The revelation that the camera could see through The Harrow was not something he would have stumbled across in his lifetime.

Nor would I, if I hadn't been forced up into that ship. I was as hopeless a romantic as he, and I'd killed him. Maybe I deserved the Harrow.

I climbed back into the cabriole and turned around, headed for the *Tiaga*'s airfield an hour away to learn what had happened to the air marshals.

THE RING OF HOURS AND SECONDS

Toten stared at Thierra. His wife sat at the kitchen table, spinning a teacup with her fingers, not meeting his eyes, her mouth pulled down in a light frown. She still wore last night's dress, though it was mid-morning, and she looked exhausted.

"How much did you lose this time?" he asked. His eyes drifted up to the small window behind the sink, looking out at another window into another drab kitchen a few feet away. A bouquet of dead flowers that Thierra had gathered weeks ago sat in a vase near the window. Dried, yellow petals had puddled on the counter beneath it.

For an excellent thief, one of the best, he should have been able to afford a flat significantly higher in the city. But until Thierra stopped gambling, they lived near the mud-choked streets.

"I almost won," she said with a trace of defiance and frustration in her voice. "If that fat old Mr. Sochett hadn't cheated, I'd have cleaned house. I was this close!"

There was movement in the corner of his eye, but Toten didn't look at her. No doubt, she held up her fingers, pinched with the first finger and thumb almost touching. *This close*. It was always this close.

"How much?"

"A hundred thousand," she said sheepishly.

This time he did look at her, his head snapping around, but she was staring into her teacup as if it might reveal the winner of an upcoming horse race, or the next card, or the next roll of the dice.

"A hundred thousand?" He sagged against the counter and tried to swallow, but his throat had suddenly gone dry.

"I was up eighty thousand," she said.

"That doesn't do us any good, does it?"

She leaned back and rubbed her neck. "What are we gonna do?" It was always *we* when she lost.

His breath wheezed in and out as he tried to think. "I got thirty thousand from my share of that last job at the docks. That would have dug us out. There aren't any other big jobs coming up."

She twisted the belt on her skirt. She was twisting hard.

"What?" he said.

"Mr. Beraghar holds the debt. He said we have to pay within the week, and if we don't have the money, he has a job for you."

"You gambled at one of *Beraghar's* houses?" he sputtered, fully facing her now and gripping the back of the empty kitchen chair. Mr. Beraghar should have gone to the guild of Masons and Builders with his request. The guild assigned thieves. That Mr. Beraghar was going through Thierra meant the guild had turned him down. Certain jobs were too dangerous or political for the guild to accept.

"He said it'll clear the books."

Toten turned back to the dirty kitchen window. In the other kitchen, a wife in a housecoat and yellow belt walked past carrying a pot. "It'll clear the books? A hundred thousand just like that? You know that means it's going to be ugly. Probably something against the Baron." *Something that could get Toten killed.*

"I don't know what else to do! We can pay him the thirty thousand, and you can borrow the rest from the guild maybe?"

"I'm already paying off the forty thousand I borrowed for you last month."

She shrank on herself. "I'm sorry," she said. "I wanted to cash out, but I was winning."

"Of course, you were! They let you win, drove up the stakes, and then took you down. It's what they do." He stopped. He'd told her this a hundred times, but sometimes she won big and so he knew she didn't believe the game was rigged. She once won so much she'd bought a proper steam car and a dozen sets of driving clothes and rented a cottage on the far side of the city for six months. The car was long returned to pay debts, and the clothes were packed away for want of a vehicle to drive.

He shrugged into his vest and coat, there was no point in going out if you didn't look proper. "I'll talk to Mr. Beraghar."

She leapt to her feet. "Oh, thank you."

"Don't thank me until we know what the job is."

"I promise I won't gamble again. This time I mean it. I promise."

"I know." Toten kissed her on the cheek, and she hugged him back fiercely, fingers digging into the back of his coat.

Toten walked three blocks to the corner of Grace and Mast where there was a pneumatic lift up to the upper tiers. From there, he could rent an airlift to Mr. Beraghar's lofty apartment at the highest tier in the city of towers. How high could you build? No one knew. The engineers swore they could build higher, but Toten figured the question would only be settled on the day that one of those towers fell. Down here in the depths, the engineers had installed massive steel columns, latticework beams, and arches, often right through the existing shanties and old apartments.

At least they were kind enough not to raze the buildings. They just drove the piles right down through them and let the lower folks live with massive beams running out of their windows. Gotta duck on your way to the toilet. It had happened to one of Toten's childhood friends, who swore he cracked his head on the beam in his living room twice a day. At least he got fresh eggs from the pigeons nesting in the flanges.

Toten crowded onto the lift with dozens of other low-dwellers, all dressed nicely on their way to jobs higher up. Waiters and stewards. The lift had no railing, just a wooden platform on tracks, but Toten figured if he got pushed off, he could leap for a window or a washing line passing by. After a lifetime of thieving, he automatically scanned for escape routes. He knew he did it, but it was second nature.

At the upper tier, he trudged off with other men. The rest continued on to the upper-upper tier. There was an upper-upper-upper tier above that, called the Triple-Ups, and Toten thought the people who named things ought to put more thought into it.

At the balloon-docking station, throat tight and stomach nauseous, he asked for Mr. Beraghar's apartment. "Two hundredth level, St. Aupert's," he said to the old balloon man. St. Aupert's was a private island of tall buildings unconnected to the pneumatics in the rest of the city.

"I can get you to the landing dock at one-seventy-five," the stooped, minimally toothed old man said, pulling on his flatcap. "You'll go through their security from there."

"Of course."

The old man checked a couple of dials on his tanks, unleashed fire, and the balloon lurched up on guidewires. Toten gripped the basket as buildings sped past. Twice, the old driver slowed at a crossing and switched wires, nimbly moving horizontally as well as vertically, passing other balloons of varying sizes. The last crossing, a wire of thousands of feet long between the building cluster at Horitz Street and the cluster at St. Aupert's, was the demarcation between buildings connected to the city system, and St. Aupert's that chose not to be. Thieves didn't steal from St. Aupert's.

"There she is," the old man said, nodding to the soaring arches and carved wood of St. Aupert's highest tower as it approached.

Toten nodded and looked away. He stared instead at the vast city sprawling below and around him, from the docks, to Senate Hill, to the tree-lined, low western suburbs. He knew it all intimately. The sun gleamed off the endless eastern ocean, but Toten had no interest in travel or ships. The city was all the world he needed.

He noted the cluster of black buildings to the southwest. Rumor was that some idiot had released a demon a hundred years ago, turning the old Mukrove towers dark. They said it had never

been the same inside since, even with the demon banished —
madness and whatnot. Toten didn't believe any of it. Occultists
lived there now, quite happy for its notoriety. Thieves didn't
generally rob Mukrove either, because of its reputation and
because most Occulties didn't have anything worth stealing.

And in between St. Aupert's and Mukrove stood clusters and
islands of buildings on a massive scale, two-hundred-plus
stories high, basking in clear air and sunny skies. Most of the high
buildings had promenades and sundecks where the great people
of society lounged in opulence. Thieves were very interested in
those buildings, and Toten figured he'd robbed them all at one
point or another. He longed to bask up there with them in peace,
just once.

The balloon came gently into the landing platform at St.
Aupert's on Level 175, and they were met by four gentlemen in
long coats with guns holstered at their hips.

"Business?" said the largest of them, a bullnosed man with
shaved head who had probably been a low-level cop once given
the number of scars on his face.

"I need an audience with Mr. Beraghar," Toten said. "He's
asked to see me. Toten Haday."

Bullnose marched to an earpiece on a nearby wall while his
three compatriots didn't move away from staring.

"Lovely day, isn't it?" Toten said to them. "You can see for
miles." He walked to the railing at the lip of the platform and his
neck crawled. It wouldn't be hard for them to heave him over.

It really did smell nice up here without the sewage and coal
smoke.

"You're in luck," Bullnose called. "He'll see you. Mr. Gentle
will escort you up."

Toten waved at the balloon man, who slipped his moorings
and slid away down the wire, then joined the skinny man called
Mr. Gentle on a very small lift that pressed them shoulder to
shoulder. Toten didn't care for that. At least the curved front was
glass, so he could watch the city spread out around him. So many
places to rob. Most buildings had different personalities and

income levels, but fads came and went. Old stodgy clusters might spring to life again with a new generation of wealth looking to get out from under the eyes of their parents.

"Mr. Beraghar don't normally accept guests," Mr. Gentle said conversationally. "Are you important? Important people don't usually come up the balloons."

"I'm not important. It's about a debt."

"A lot of people owe Mr. Beraghar money. Like I said, he don't normally accept guests."

"I'm as in the dark as you are."

"He's a bit of a slob, he is."

"What?"

"He's a bit of terrible slob. He'll probably meet you in the front room, that's the only one that's presentable. I had to go in once after he and his men had a row with one of the other lords, blood everywhere, I can tell you, and it was a pigsty." Mr. Gentle shook his head, obviously more disturbed by the mess than the blood. "He could buy and sell every cleaning house in the city, but he doesn't let people up very often. Food, plates, teacups, clothes. Everywhere."

Toten grimaced. "Hopefully you won't need to come collect my body."

"See that I don't. Don't want to go in there again."

The lift stopped and Toten stepped off on a private landing platform that fronted a grand, wooden door with iron bands. Three marble steps led up to the door, which was ridiculous as the apartment was on the level and didn't need steps. Was the whole apartment raised up? What was under the floor then? He mulled the possibilities.

"Mind your tongue and see that I don't have to come up," Mr. Gentle reminded as he closed the glass door and dropped from view.

No point in waiting. Toten skipped up the steps and knocked with the ridiculously large and grotesque knocker. A well-dressed manservant answered.

"Wait here," he said, bringing Toten into a vast entry vestibule that towered three stories high and supported many windows.

Warm sunlight poured in across elegant portraits of couples in the clothes of different eras. They looked exactly like the portraits on the walls of old families—parents and grandparents and great-grandparents going back nauseatingly far—only Mr. Beraghar was the first wealthy man in his lineage. People from the lower levels didn't have paintings of ancestors.

"Toten Haday, husband of Thierra Haday," boomed a large voice as a large man with a large beard bustled through one of several doors at the rear of the vestibule. His bespoke gray suit looked ridiculously expensive to Toten's practiced eye. A moment later, two bodyguards of even more impressive size followed through the door.

"Mr. Beraghar," he said. "I'm terribly sorry about Thierra last night. She got in over her head and I've come up to offer my sincerest apologies."

"Have you come to pay?"

"I have thirty thousand, and I can get the rest shortly. I'm good for it."

"Thirty thousand is not a hundred thousand."

"Yes, sir. My wife told me there might be a job I could do that would help resolve this problem."

Mr. Beraghar eyed him and stroked his beard. The bodyguards said nothing. "You come well recommended," he said. "I asked around, and it sounds like you could be more successful if you wanted to be. Your wife is holding you back."

"Yes, sir, but what's a man to do?"

"Then you're a sentimental fool. Sooner or later her debts will catch up to her, you know. It's inevitable. Ask my first two wives." He smiled. "Well, it's your choice. If she ends up dead in an alley some night, come talk to me about permanent employment."

"Thank you." Toten replied tightly. He didn't want to think of Thierra dead. It wasn't her fault, she had a compulsion, and he would always steal his way out of her troubles. Love was love. "What can I humbly help you with? My skills only go so far."

"That's not what I hear. Come with me." Mr. Beraghar strode past and exited through the grand front door. One bodyguard followed, and one waited for Toten.

Toten joined Mr. Beraghar at the railing of the landing platform. The bodyguards stood too close and he kept very aware of where they stood.

"That's the mark there. The Mukrove Towers." Mr. Beraghar pointed at the dark towers in the distance.

Toten winced. "Thieves don't go there."

"Of course they don't. It would be silly, right? There's madness and ghosts in those apartments. You're going anyway."

Toten inhaled and exhaled. "What's the job?" What could possibly be worth a hundred thousand in there?"

"There's a necromancer on the 143rd Floor named Nekravé, which I'm certain is a made-up name. I'm not even sure if they're a man or woman due to all the dark robes and theatrics, but they've got something interesting, and I'd like you to steal it."

"What is the object of interest?"

"It's a ring, which Nekravé wears on their middle finger. A clock ring. Nekravé is one of only a few living necromancers to have made one, and I want it."

Toten turned to face the man fully. "You want me to go into the Mukrove Towers, get to the 143rd Floor, break into a necromancer's apartment, and steal a *ring*?"

"Yes."

"Is this a gold ring, studded with jewels?"

"It's an iron ring, studded with gears. It looks uncomfortable."

"How's that worth anything at all?"

"That's my business."

"Well, does it do something? Or shoot something?"

"Again, my business." Mr. Beraghar's voice turned threatening.

"I need to know if it'll hurt me when I pick it up."

"The answer is no."

Toten nodded.

Mr. Beraghar continued. "Nekravé goes out for tea every Wednesday at the Shrop Hanger Restaurant with several other necromancers, and they never wear the ring. I hear it's considered impolite and boastful. That is your opportunity to get into their safe, and you'll have over an hour."

"There'll be necromancer guards on the building."

Mr. Beraghar waved dismissively. "Are you superstitious?"

"I'm not, but necromancer guards are uncannily dangerous. So I've heard."

"You are a master thief. Act like it."

"Fine. But what if I'm caught? What happens to Thierra?"

"Her debt will be forgiven if you succeed and only if you succeed, so don't fail. If you get caught and give up my name, it'll go even worse for her."

Toten grimaced. He did not like Mr. Beraghar, but Thierra had put him in a difficult situation.

Mr. Beraghar threw an arm around his shoulders and squeezed. "What do you think, Mr. Haday? Can you do it?"

"Does the sun rise and set without fail? Does God love this, the greatest city in the world? Of course I can do it. What's your timetable?"

"Two weeks."

"That's too tight."

"Two weeks."

Toten pictured Thierra sitting at the kitchen table. Necromancers terrified her, as did most anything occult, but Mr. Beraghar was a known threat. "Fine."

Mr. Beraghar turned back to the view, arm still around Toten's shoulders. "It is the greatest city in the world, isn't it?"

Toten returned to his same, tired kitchen. This time, he sat at the table with his hands around a teacup while Thierra paced. She was pale, and her sharp eyes were dark. The dried flowers had lost more petals.

"Tell me what Mr. Beraghar wants you to do."

"No."

"Tell me!"

"It doesn't matter. He wants something, he's going to get it."

"Is it dangerous?"

"I don't know yet."

She stopped pacing and hugged herself, looking small. "This is all my fault."

"Come here." He slid his chair back and she sat on his lap, wrapping herself around him, burying her face in his neck. He felt the dampness of her tears against his throat. "They wanted me for a job, so they set you up. Mr. Beraghar has people who do that." He rubbed her back gently. "We'll get through this."

"But what if something happens to you?"

"I'm the best there is. You believe that, don't you?"

She nodded.

"Then we'll get through this."

"Just tell me the job."

"I can't. I know you won't tell, but the walls have ears. Now jump off." She slipped off his lap and he stood. "I have to plan, and that means I'm going to be late for the next bunch of nights. I don't want you gambling. Right? No gambling…"

"I don't have any money."

"Let me hear you say it."

"I won't gamble. Happy?"

"Of course I'm happy. I'm always happy with you."

She pulled him in for another tight hug and kissed him. "I can't sit around doing nothing," she said. "I'll go back to my job at Marta's."

"That's good. They need help."

Sometime later, he stood on the third-floor balcony of a shuttered restaurant, looking across at the start of the Mukrove city block. Several shops were boarded up, but most were doing fine. Mukrove itself seemed a lively enough place, and people came and went in a continuous trickle, so the dark rumors weren't keeping people away.

There were five towers in the complex, all the color of old ash, but only two of them soared to great heights. Who sunned themselves on the topmost decks? A number of midsized and lesser buildings filled the spaces in between, and a park meandered around them all. The park had been let grow wild, with vines and creepers coating the trees and lampposts and the lower stories of the buildings in an explosion of growth. It seemed almost planned for ambiance.

He looked toward the front door of the target tower. He'd want to get to know the cleaning staff and maintenance men. Maybe apply for a job. He'd watch Nekravé and get to know their patterns and personality.

Should he rent a balloon and drift across the buildings to get a higher view? As dangerous as necromancers were, they were still human with the usual failings, weaknesses, and vanities. He'd be fine. Thierra would be fine.

Two weeks was tight for a difficult job, though.

Mr. Beraghar must want the ring quickly for a reason. Toten would also have to scout out his new employer. There was no point in succeeding and then getting stabbed from behind after the job was done. He needed to know what the ring was for.

Two weeks later, just after three-thirty in the afternoon on Wednesday, Toten stumbled from a street-trolley into his favorite steak house, a long way from the Mukrove Towers. The iron clock ring lay cradled in his pocket, jabbing him with an edge.

Clouds of steam billowed from the kitchen, and the place smelled deliciously of cooking meat, but he was cold and couldn't concentrate. Today, the smell and the sizzling, the calling cooks and waiters, had no impact.

He wiped sweat from his forehead. How could people live in those towers? There was truth to the madness that people whispered about. It hung thick. The walls and air were tainted with it, smelling of old lilacs. How did they stand it? He'd spent two weeks working there and he would never go back.

He'd get this ring to Mr. Beraghar and be done with it. He didn't want a celebratory steak, he wanted a scalding bath, but steak was what he did every time. It was his good-luck habit.

An impeccably dressed waiter with a festive, yellow hand-kerchief in his breast pocket brought a rare steak and a potato. Toten began sawing at them with little attention. Then the sound and atmosphere in the room shifted. He'd spent his life listening to ambiance, and he looked up as a familiar, dark robed figure swung around him and pulled out the empty chair at his table. He backed away quickly as people openly stared. Nekravé's hood swung loose and low, preventing him from getting a look at their face above a strong chin, vanishingly pale lips, and a hint of shiny copper.

He'd watched them long enough to recognize their limp.

"You've taken something important and made me cross this whole forsaken city chasing you," Nekravé said in an obviously fake, obviously annoyed, sepulchral accent.

"I don't know what you're talking about," Toten said firmly, preparing to bolt for the door.

Nekravé peered down at Toten's plate. "How can you eat that?" they said. "It looks revolting. I'm a vegetarian."

Before he could reply, Nekravé raised a closed fist, opened it, and blew powder at his face.

Toten coughed violently, and his vision dimmed.

He awoke, slumped, strapped to a chair in a stuffy, dimly lit room. It took a few minutes to gather his thoughts. How much time had passed? The room held an unsettled atmosphere that he recognized like an itch at the back of his throat, and he shuddered at the smell of lilacs.

He finally shook off the drugs, and his eyes fastened on a collection of brass and wooden instruments hanging on a disturbingly red wall to his right. Sexual implements? Each hand-held device, with its leather bindings, clamps, pistons, and coiled, braided steam-hoses, had been lovingly polished and displayed to prominent effect. He jerked his eyes away in terror, looking around, but the small room held nothing else except his chair, the table before him, and two sputtering gas-lamps on the wall. Their uneven hiss the only sound.

He yanked at the straps that bound his arms, but they were too tight to reach the buckles. No worry—he'd be a poor thief if he couldn't escape a binding. He had to hurry. Nekravé would return soon, that was certain.

With a twist of his hand, a small blade on a spring leapt through the fabric of his sleeve cuff. He began sawing at the thick strap, making quick progress, breathing rhythmically to keep from panicking. Got to keep control, or he was lost. That was a motto and a lifestyle. In moments, the strap was through, and he tugged at the buckle on his opposite wrist. Then to the shin-straps.

It may have only been thirty seconds, but that was too long. Got to go. He leapt to his feet and dodged around the table. Hesitating at the door, he listened, then pulled it open. Of course, Nekravé stood right there in the corridor, black-robed, reaching for the doorknob. Without hesitation, Toten charged into them, knocking them back, sprinting down the corridor for the stairs. Nekravé did not shout or say a word, but he felt them following. How close? How fast could a limping necromancer realistically run in robes?

He'd memorized the layout of the building, and each floor was the same. A corridor in a loop around the core, apartments outside the loop and elevators and stairs inside. The same burgundy patterned carpet lay on every floor, worn into tracks after so many years, and wall sconces cast flickering light from small gas flames. Time to take the stairs.

If Nekravé was smart, they'd take the elevator and try to catch him at the bottom of the building, so he'd run up instead.

He burst into the stairs, noting the floor number in tile on the wall—143—and ran up, keeping the slap of his shoes on the stair treads to a minimum. He had energy, he had breath, he could run a long distance. He didn't hear the door of the stairwell crash open beneath him, so Nekravé must have chosen the elevator. Good. Now where to get off? He'd scouted the underused landing platform at 154 last week.

A short time later, his lungs heaving, he came to a stop on the landing at 154. His headache was worse, not better, but he tried to listen over his own gasping. There were no voices calling beyond the door, no one obviously waiting. If he could get to the cables that the balloons used, he could initiate a daring and stupid escape.

How had Nekravé followed him? Could they do it again?

He'd have to lay low for a while and find another way to appease Mr. Beraghar. He'd check in with the Thieves' Guild and let them know about this whole cock-up. Nekravé might lodge a complaint.

He took the smooth, bronze doorknob out to the landing platform and pulled. Nekravé stood there outside, hand extended, and threw powder into his face.

Toten awoke, strapped to a chair in a brightly lit, stuffy room. His head was slumped forward, and he had a terrible headache. He didn't recognize anything, but he felt like he'd been here before. What had happened?

His eyes fastened on the brass devices displayed on a disturbingly red wall to his right. Sexual implements? He had to get out of here! He jerked his eyes away and looked around, assessing, but the small room held nothing else but his chair, a table, and four sputtering gas-lamps.

He yanked at the straps that bound his arms, then twisted his wrist. Nothing happened. What? Looking down, he saw a fresh hole in his sleeve, but the blade was not there. Fear settled in his heart.

The door opened as he was unsuccessfully trying to get his hip-blade to flip out. Nekravé entered carrying a straight-backed, wooden chair. They placed it across from him and sank onto it while Toten made his expression deliberately calm.

As before, Nekravé's face was only visible from the tip of their nose down to their chin.

"Please stop cutting through my leather," they said in that same oddly fake sepulchral voice. "It's expensive to replace."

"What are you talking about? I haven't cut anything."

They shrugged lightly and held up their slender, pale hand, revealing the black, iron clock-ring with all its gears and angles on their middle finger. "This is the third time we've done this dance, though you won't remember the first two. In both of those prior times you revealed a cleverly hidden blade and cut through my straps. I've relieved you of both of those blades. Please stop."

"You drugged me and took my memory?"

"No drugs, except for the sleeping dust. This clock-ring has many attributes, one of which is to reverse time. You escaped, I knocked you out and reversed time, and here we begin again. Only I can remember this reversal, as I am the ring-holder. For you, this is the first time you've been here except that you're lighter a pair of blades."

Toten stared at the ring in consternation. Magic wasn't real. He assumed Nekravé was lying, and she'd drugged him. "No wonder people want that ring," he said half-jokingly. "Reversing time? The things a thief could do with that."

"Yes, they could, I suppose. That's not its purpose."

Toten leaned back, feeling around for his ankle knife as fear began to set in. He looked at the array of devices hanging on the wall, then back into the impenetrable cowl. "What happens next?"

Nekravé started shaking slightly, and it took a moment for Toten to realize they were laughing. "Those aren't for you, silly. Those are mine, and I hang them there for remembrance."

"Yours?"

"We could take them down to play, if you like."

"No."

They reached up gently and lifted their cowl from their face to reveal horrific damage. Half of Nekravé's face was metal. Toten twitched, then stilled his expression again.

Nekravé was a woman, at least he thought she was, thin to gauntness. Nearly the entire side of her head and face had been replaced with sculpted copper. Her hairline stopped abruptly above her right eyebrow, and half of that eyebrow was gone. Her temple, ear, and cheek had been replaced with polished metal; her right eye was a bronze artifice, turning in its socket, mechanical pupil dilating and adjusting; her neck tendons were delicate pistons that disappeared down into her black robes where the shoulder seemed to be artifice too. The flesh of her forehead and cheek were raw where they met metal.

"Do you like it?" she said, tilting her head.

"Whoever did the work is amazing," he said, refusing to turn away. "Best I've seen."

"I was an artist at the highest levels before the accident. People paid great sums to watch me perform, so I could afford the best artificers."

Toten squinted, looking at her, and then at the wall of toys, comprehension dawning. "You were a courtesan?"

"I was an artist!" She half rose and then sat again. "I was an artist, until a steam cannister exploded. The damage was significant to my body and my brain. Wealth can only repair so much, but I survived. I can no longer perform, but I've acquired an alternate viewpoint on life and its excesses in the highest towers."

"That's when you became a necromancer?"

She nodded, the pistons in her neck extending and retracting noiselessly. There was gold inlay to complete her truncated eyebrow, and delicate filigree to recreate the look of a jawbone.

"I'm forever trapped between life and death," she said, "so why not worship at its altar?"

Toten shifted, uncomfortable with her blasphemy. "What do you want of me?" First Mr. Beraghar, now this mad necromancer. He was not used to being blackmailed, but he would listen to her demands.

"I could kill you," she said. Her fake accent had dropped, and she had a typical educated woman's accent of the north quadrant. "The guild won't protect you. You stole outside of sanction, and worse—you got caught."

"Or?" Toten prompted, waiting.

"I want you to explore a new piece of the necromantic realm while I sit here in safety."

"Necromantic realm?"

"You've never heard of it?"

"I make a point of not prying into necromancer business."

"Until now, that is? At its simplest, it is a parallel world of darkness and shadows. There are places of great value in it, at least to necromancers. There are libraries left by the ancient ones, tombs of powerful demons, and creatures made of darkness."

"Sounds lovely." It sounded like a bad hallucination. "So I just scout out the place, and then I can go?"

"Of course. I'll have no more need of you. You've already told me Mr. Beraghar is your employer."

Toten jerked forward. "I never told you that."

"In one of the other two times you were here, when I was torturing you on this table, you sang like a bird."

"I don't believe you."

"I don't care."

Toten looked around for any chance of escape. The gas lamps hissed, the tools on the wall looked even more frightening now, and the atmosphere of the room weighed on him. He didn't want to be drugged and at her mercy.

"What do I have to do if I say yes?"

"Oh good," she said, half smiling with the human side of her face. "I knew you'd be reasonable."

"What do I do?"

"I've developed a new door into the necromantic realm, one that leads much higher up in the scale if I'm right."

"What does that mean?"

"It doesn't matter, I just need you to go in and come back and tell me what you saw. I think you'll be dizzyingly high, far away from all existing doors. A new place entirely. A new zone on the map." She clasped her hands together excitedly. "I could win an award at the annual banquet."

"Just go in, come back, and tell you what I saw?" He'd play along and pretend he saw something. The explosion had obviously damaged her brain.

"Yes."

"And what are the odds of my head getting bitten off by one of those beasts you mentioned?"

"High. But the odds of you screaming to death on this table are also high."

"So, I don't have a choice."

"Of course you have a choice. And if you go in, whether you survive or not, I'll make sure your wife's debt is settled. Is that fair?"

Despite his fear of what was about to happen, Toten felt a flush of relief. "Fair. Where's this door then? What do I need to smoke or inhale? Is there prep work?"

"Not like that." She held up the clock-ring again. "This is the door, and it's far more complex than the older, existing rings, I can tell you that. I'm quite proud."

"That's a door?" he said doubtfully. Maybe she'd already introduced some sort of gas into the room to make him hallucinate. Was it already too late?

Nekravé nodded eagerly. "We have dozens of rings like this—simple and more limited in their function, and they're all doors." She pointed to the largest gear poking out from the side, its fine teeth curving back into the black face of the ring. "This is the wheel of hours. It was how I reversed time to catch you. Below it are additional gears and wheels—minutes and seconds, obviously. In between those are smaller and smaller wheels. They allow you to slip between minutes, cut between seconds. The spaces that get forgotten. You know about those spaces, don't you? You live in those spaces. Places where no one sees or hears. A lot of people live in those spaces and the city forgets them. That's as true for your world as it is for mine."

"There are hiding spaces between seconds?" He wasn't following her logic.

"This ring is special because of the quantity and quality of the gears. I can cut the seconds finer, slipping into smaller spaces. I will go places no one has ever gone."

"You mean *I'll* go."

"It's a noble sacrifice. There are necromancers whom we call Lamplighters. They find safe paths through the darkness. I would be a Lamplighter to my people, but it doesn't do anyone any good if I'm killed while doing it. So, it's a time-honored practice to use proxies for our explorations. Others have gone before you, others will follow—some are successful, and some are not.

"Now what do you say?" She rustled her robes and looked expectant. "Are you going to do this, or do I begin dissecting you? I need a willing participant."

"Are you a monster?"

"I'm an artist."

He stared into her human eye for a long moment, and she didn't blink. She was so utterly convinced of this that he began to get nervous. "Where will I be when I go through the door? I won't go without some idea of what to expect." If he was going to make up visions for her, he needed to know what she expected him to see.

"I'll describe it in terms you can understand but know that it isn't like this at all. These are approximations. You'll see darkness at first, and the air will be hot and dry. You'll be standing on gritty soil, with vague impressions of bushes and trees around you." Nekravé closed her human eye. Her open, bronze eye continued to turn in its mechanical socket. "It's night with no moon, and the stars are not our constellations. Your eyes will adjust enough to see the ruins of houses scattered around you. That seems to be typical for the city."

She was taking this seriously. He had an itch between his shoulder blades. "How big are the houses? How close together?"

She opened her eye. "One or two stories, wood-framed, spaced apart. It doesn't matter, you can't explore them. There are eyes on you from every window. Not long after, the dogs will come." Her gaze was far away. "They're not dogs, of course, but how else do you describe the indescribable except with familiar names."

Toten fought laughter at her naivete and gullibility. "Am I looking for anything specific?"

"Light. You're looking for one of the rare houses that are lit brilliantly. There are a few in town, and the town is vast. They're library houses. You can't avoid the dogs, but they don't like the light. If you can get to one of those houses, you'll be safe." She waved her hand with the iron ring. "Successful rings open doors close to those houses and give us safe access, unsuccessful ones lead to darkness and therefore death."

"I hope your ring works."

"It will." She kissed the ring and held it up. "There's a mountain—you can see it by the hollow lack of stars and a couple of bright houses scattered across it. There's a single beacon at its peak. That is the house we're aiming for." She shivered.

"Has anyone gone up there before?"

"How could they? They don't have my ring." She stood. "Time to go."

"Now?" He jerked against the straps.

She came around the table, tugged off the ring, and slid it onto his finger. She leaned over and began twisting wheels and gears. "Have you ever left the city before?"

"No, why would I?"

"You're in for a treat. I've put thirty seconds on the timer." She stood, and he noticed that the arm on her damaged side seemed shorter. "That's this button here." She pointed to a tiny button on the ring's edge.

"Thirty seconds isn't much time."

"It's too much time in there. Remember, you're cutting through the seconds, elongating them. The dogs will come, so start running immediately. Zig and zag, don't run in a straight line. I hope you return."

He stared at the rotating gears in the ring, transfixed. He could hear it ticking, counting the seconds. Three… four… five…

"Don't steal anything," she called, stepping to the wall. "Also, ignore the voices and don't read the books. Both can drive you mad if you don't know what you're doing."

"Voices?"

The room suddenly began to tremble with a nauseating hum, and the gas lamps dimmed. … Seven… eight… nine… Toten yanked at the straps again, hurting himself.

"Thirty seconds—but the seconds are bigger there. Good luck."

The room vanished.

Toten snapped open his eyes and it was, as described, very dark. He was standing, no longer bound, and the air was thick, hot, and prickly, and it stank of mildew. Where was he? He spun, disoriented, his boots scraping on sand. The bushes she'd spoken of moved unnaturally in his peripheral vision. Some were as big as trees, restlessly contorting. He couldn't focus his eyes on them. A half-collapsed house loomed beyond them in the darkness and an intense feeling of being watched grew. There were voices at the edge of hearing. This couldn't be real. He was hallucinating. Turning his head, he found the double-gabled mansion that Nekravé wanted, the only source of light in this place. It was up a steep hill. It was not close.

Fear clawed at him, but he had to do this for Thierra. Damn Nekravé.

He heard a noise and dove and rolled without hesitation and came up running at a sprint, boots chewing into the sandy ground. He dodged right and curved back left, terror driving his legs as hard as they'd ever gone.

Darkness leapt at him, and he felt searing pain across his back. He stumbled but kept running. Light meant safety! Nekravé had said so.

How far uphill? A hundred and fifty feet? They were right on him, the dogs with snapping jaws, when he burst across the last gap, hurtling up the steps onto the front porch, slamming into the front wall of the house between a window and the door. He spun to face them, but there was nothing there—just barren soil sloping steeply away. He hesitantly returned to the top of the steps, panting and sweating in the heat. The light only reached so far, and he saw great bodies of darkness pacing beyond the circle of light, glaring with wolfish eyes.

His presence was resented.

"This isn't real," he said, begging himself to believe it. "Come on, hold yourself together. She drugged me. Wait it out, it'll end soon." The whispering voices swelled and fell, the susurrus of a crowd, and if he listened hard, he could almost understand them.

He gingerly pulled his coat off and stuck his hand through the slashes in the back then tossed it over the porch railing. Next, he peeled off his vest. It was damp with blood. Probing with his fingers, he didn't think the cuts were that deep. He'd survived worse. He put the vest back on and buttoned it, wincing.

"You're too slow," he yelled out, but his voice fell feebly in the heavy air. "I'm not a paunchy necromancer in flouncy robes." He felt their surge of anger and a deep growl arose from the darkness farther down the hill. A hundred throats took it up, and the furious rumble moved slowly from left to right.

Trembling, he lifted the clock-ring to the light, inhaling a shaky breath. Was it ticking? It wasn't ticking, and he felt cold panic despite the heat. Suddenly, it clicked, the gear moving once, and then it stopped again. He shook it next to his ear. What had she said about seconds lasting longer? Damn her. How long was a second? He counted almost to seventy before the clock ticked again. It was still moving, and he felt a rush of relief.

He stared out at the pacing, growling dogs. It was real. It felt *too* real. Necromancers were fools to come here.

He lowered the ring and took his bearings, struggling to ignore the noise and smell that were burrowing into his head. The porch was limned in warped and peeling boards, once white, but it was otherwise empty of rocking chairs and potted plants. It disappeared around the far corner of the house into darkness.

She said he shouldn't steal here. Screw that. There were libraries in these houses, but was there anything actually worth taking?

Glancing out one last time, he couldn't help himself, he noted the pinpricks of light far below him. The other beacon houses down on the plain. The strange constellations above and the lights below might have been beautiful in another place.

He felt blood on his back, hot on his spine.

Turning, he pushed through the front door into an oddly barren foyer. Dark wainscotting wrapped the lower walls, and plaster peeled above in disturbing patterns. Everything blazed with light, like the porch. It came from everywhere and nowhere.

He closed the front door, muting the relentless growling, but now he heard scratching in the walls instead. Mice?

There were three closed doors across the foyer from him and a narrow stair going up. Something wet and nasty had been dragged down the stairs, leaving a thick, rancid smear. Toten tore his eyes away.

Keep moving. Keep moving.

The clock-ring ticked again.

The doorknobs of the three interior doors were plain brass, and he gripped one gingerly with his fingertips, heart thumping. The door opened into a brightly lit, front drawing room with blackened windows out to darkness.

The air in the room was hot to breathe, and he could feel the rising and falling growl through the walls, but nothing moved here. He stepped across the threshold.

There were bookshelves, packed with huge leather tomes with no titles on their spines, but what captured his attention were two tables, about six feet to a side. Each supported an elaborate model of a village. Bright lanterns on tracks hung from the crumbling, blue ceiling above each.

He edged slowly up to the first table. It held amazing detail at such a tiny scale. There was a cluster of maybe fifty wattle-and-daub huts, each about as tall as his first knuckle, all slightly different, gathered around the banks of a muddy river. He'd seen drawings of places like these in grade school. There were gardens in miniature behind each hut, and broader fields beyond. It looked so realistic that the river could have been flowing. It even looked like there were smudges of smoke rising above the huts. He leaned forward. Were the people and animals moving? He gasped and reared back, then leaned forward again. They were! But at such a tiny scale that they were moving incredibly slowly.

The animatronics must have been assembled with a jeweler's loop; they were only half as big as his pinky nail.

Why were they built, and why here?

He turned to the second table, which held a town on the low slopes of a fake, rocky mountain, whose sheer rise ended abruptly about three feet above the table. There was a crystal blue lake in front of the village, and vibrant, green meadows. Squinting, he could see the tiny animatronic people and animals and carts moving here too. Circling the table, he studied the wooden struts and plaster that held up the back of the hollow mountain. From the front, the illusion was complete. Beneath the table, there was a small lamp on tracks. The moon? Looking up, he realized that the brighter sun-lantern was moving slowly along the ceiling track.

There was nothing worth stealing here, and the siffling heat was getting to him. The scratching in the walls seemed louder and his back throbbed. The ring ticked.

Wiping his face with a handkerchief, he hurried back to the foyer and hesitantly opened the second door. A dim, narrow hallway led down to the rear of the house. There had been pictures on the stained wallpaper once, he could see the pale squares where they had hung, and there was a yellow ball on the floor, halfway down.

He traversed the corridor as quickly and as quietly as he could, neck crawling. An empty kitchen with blackened windows lay on the right. There were smeared stains across every countertop and an empty dog crate on the floor. He wasn't about to open the cabinets or larder. The other room off the corridor had probably been a dining room. Three tables with models took up the space where the dining table would have stood. The wooden buildings in the models were taller here and built much closer together. These were large towns, with narrow lanes and tenement buildings, and a few grandiose governmental buildings at the center. One had a bustling market wrapped around a fountain, with hundreds of tiny people shopping. Another had progressed beyond donkey carts into steam cars and trolleys.

He shook his head. It made no sense.

The corridor was just as oppressive and nerve-racking the second time, so that he practically ran back to the foyer.

The third door off the foyer led to the other front room. Here, there were five smaller tables crammed together. An island village dotted with strange trees caught his attention. He'd read about tropical islands. Boards had been nailed around the edges of the table to hold water, and when he dabbed in his finger, it came away wet. A fan powered by some unknown mechanism sat on a nearby stool and blew rippling waves across the tiny ocean.

Scanning across the ever-present bookshelves and black windows, he thought he saw movement beyond the glass, so he returned to the foyer again and confronted the stairs. Did he really want to go up? The stairs felt different somehow, like a threshold he shouldn't cross. The ring had ticked another three or four times, he could just wait it out here, right? The scratching in the walls grew louder, following him.

But he'd never backed down before, so using all his skill to keep silent on the creaky steps, he climbed and kept his feet clear of the awful smear. That same red-brown stain continued down the corridor above and turned into the rear bedroom. He wouldn't follow it further.

The front bedroom on his right held another model, he could see it from where he stood, but it didn't look like any city he'd ever seen. Soaring buildings of metal and glass stretched nearly to the ceiling. Before he could investigate, he froze at the sound of snoring in the front bedroom on the left.

Peeking in, he saw with shock an old man, beard long and gray and draped down his chest, sleeping in a chair. Someone lived in this terrible place? He wore workman's coveralls and was coated in sawdust. A table stood beside him, piled with knives and tools, bags of plaster, wood, wire, and jars of paint. There were other, larger tools hanging on the wall. A huge city was under construction to his right, and Toten was startled by its size. The table took up most of the room, with buildings rising six feet high and more. These towers rivaled the bedroom opposite, but they were made up of tiny bits of wood and iron rather than smooth metal.

His eyes alighted on boots with fat, gold buckles near the man's feet. *Finally! Here was something to steal.* He wouldn't think or ask himself why or how or even what this man was until later.

Sliding forward, breathing in shallow, smooth breaths, he listened to the snoring with his whole body. The scratching was above his head now, probably in the attic.

Under the harsh, overhead lamp, the old man's face was as pale and hard as marble, heavily lined. His eyebrows rose like wild spiders, delicately sprinkled with sawdust.

Toten crouched to take the boots, and looked up at the city's towers. He froze at this new perspective, recognizing everything. The Bayat Towers, the Frist Towers, the Huyagalla Towers. There was St. Aupert's where Mr. Beraghar lived, modelled in elaborate detail. There was his private landing platform. Toten located the Mukrove Towers, painted darker gray with splotches of black. Tiny hydraulic lifts with people on them rose from the depths to the heights. Little balloons moved on suspended wires.

Why was this man building a copy of his city? Toten stood in wonder and leaned over the model-in-progress. He knew the city, and he knew the model just as intimately. Every avenue, alley, and restaurant was here in detail. The longer he looked, the more uncanny it became until he couldn't deny that this actually *was* his city. How? He felt faint. Tiny crowds crossed at street corners while trams came and went. Cars filled the boulevards. An aeroplane circled then swooped down for a landing on the strip at the city's edge, while commuter trains trundled back and forth on elevated tracks.

He suddenly realized the snoring had stopped and he spun around. The old man's eyes were open, and Toten trembled. They were black from edge to edge, deep and swirling with stars. Eyes capable of swallowing worlds. A furrow grew along his stony forehead.

"Ha'baktha a La?" The man said in a low growl, sitting up, fury transforming his face. "Agakta lue olak!"

Toten snatched the first knife his hand came to on the table and held it forward. It was covered in glue and paint. He backed up. "Are you God? Are we toys?" Those eyes threatened to devour him. "The other cities and the island? Are they real too?"

"Bak," the old man rumbled, standing and yanking a massive carving blade off a hook on the wall.

Toten glanced once at the boots with gold buckles, then bolted, hurtling down the stairs, still avoiding every creaky board by instinct. The old man followed with a roar, careening off walls, bellowing unintelligibly.

Toten fumbled with the front door, yanked it open barely in time, and threw himself across the porch, almost tripping down the stairs. The growling of the dogs swelled into a howl when he emerged, and he slid to a stop on the dead, sandy soil, still holding the useless knife out in front of him. The old man crashed through the front door behind him and stopped on the porch, carving blade in his clenched hand.

The clock-ring ticked again — Toten felt it.

"Arraghava," the old man shouted into the night, looking over Toten's head, and the dogs roared back, driven to a frenzy. Just beyond the light, darkness roiled.

Toten dropped into a crouch against the noise, barely able to fight the urge to run… run… run anywhere. He gripped the knife so hard his hand cramped.

The old man shouted again, loud above the cacophony, and light flared from his eyes, billowing out from the house, licking the underside of sparse clouds like flame. The dogs, horrid mockeries of skinless beasts, fled before it, scrambling downhill and squirming under the porches of derelict houses. Vanishing. The voices paused.

Toten stood in awe, knees popping. He could see all now. The abandoned and haunted town sprawled down the mountain below him and across the plains like a shapeless stain with no end. But that wasn't what grabbed his attention. Giant monsters walked out there.

God-Beasts a thousand feet tall, as tall as the mountain, ambled ponderously on four legs or six. Their indifferent steps crushed houses in swaths hundreds of feet long. They were hairless, the color of livid pus, and their nightmare-faces, level with the ground where he stood, were part-human and part-insect. Heads swung back and forth slowly, half lidded eyes searching. Mandibles chewed. Below them, the lanes and alleys of the town rippled and churned with the motion of — for lack of a better word — dogs.

The old man closed his eyes and darkness dropped, leaving Toten in his small ring of light, blinking. He remained still, hoping his insignificance would save him as the susurrus of voices rose again. The old man strode back inside and slammed the door.

The gear of seconds ticked.

Trembling, he lifted the clock-ring and gently clicked the gear of hours back four ticks with his fingernail.

Toten took a seat at his favorite steak house, a fresh bandage on his back. Clouds of steam billowed from the kitchen, and the place smelled wonderful. He felt cold and his hands still shook.

The clock-ring was nestled in his vest pocket where he'd shoved it when he returned, and the knife was wrapped in a newspaper at his hip. His coat was lost, still draped over the railing of the porch back at that house, so he was underdressed for the room. If he'd calculated correctly when turning the hour gear, he had taken himself back to just after his original theft.

A waiter with a red pocket handkerchief in his breast pocket brought steak and a potato, and Toten began sawing at the steak, waiting. The sudden shift in atmosphere announced that Nekravé had arrived. He looked up as the dark-robed figure pulled out the empty chair at his table, noting the slight hesitation of her copper and bronze parts.

"You've taken something important from me and made me cross this whole forsaken city chasing you," Nekravé said in her fake, sepulchral accent, just like before.

People were staring, and Toten didn't care.

He pulled a clunky iron ring out of his pants pocket, a replica he'd made a week ago, and held it up between his thumb and finger. "You told me that if this didn't work, it was useless. Well, it didn't put me at the house so it must be useless. It's mine now. I'm keeping it."

Nekravé's arrogance evaporated, and she shoved back the hood from her face. Her flesh eye was wide, the bronze eye was fixed on the ring. "What?" she said in a strong northeast quadrant, lower-class accent.

"The house was too far away. I barely outran the dogs."

"You went?" she said excitedly. "You did, I see it in your eyes, and then you shifted hours back to meet me here. Of course you did. How did you outrun the dogs?"

"A lifetime of outrunning things that mean me harm." He shivered and looked at the chatting lunch-goers. Were they all automatons? Nekravé was, by her own choice, but now that his eyes were opened, he could see the artifice binding everyone together. Rubber bands and stuffing and pistons for beating hearts. Toys of a monstrous god.

"What's inside the bright houses?" he said.

"Libraries. Books. Some we can read; some we don't dare."

"What else?"

"Nothing, why?"

So there weren't models of worlds in every house? Was this the only such house? "What does 'Arraghava' mean?"

She looked at him quizzically. "It means 'Not yet'. Where did you read that."

He shrugged.

"Oh, you have some stories to tell, don't you? Give me the ring."

"It didn't work."

"I'm not going to allow it out among you thieves, turning back hours. Give it back and tell me everything you saw. I'll let you live."

Toten drew the paint-spattered knife out of the newspaper, set the fake ring on the table, and slammed the butt of the knife down on it. It cracked and gears tumbled out. He hadn't expected it to be that easy. "There." He returned the knife to its newspaper. "It's yours."

Nekravé looked down at it in horror. "You broke it," she said in a small voice, and Toten knew that she couldn't make another. She'd intended to modify it to try again.

She jerked her closed fist up from beneath the table. He was ready. When she opened her hand and prepared to blow powder in his face, he was already blowing back. She looked startled as the blue dust hit her.

"We did this before, didn't we?" she slurred with the working half of her mouth. Her bronze eye in its mechanical socket dropped down with a click. Her shoulder slumped. She toppled forward onto the table.

He drew a handkerchief out of his breast pocket and swept the pieces of the ring into it. Two waiters hurried over.

"She'll be fine," he said. "Sleeping powder. She'll be up again in no time."

He tossed a generous sum of money on the table beside his uneaten meal and left the restaurant. The true ring was still hidden in his vest pocket.

Up above, the sun shone. He squinted, raising his hand to shield his eyes, and saw the wires and the track of the lantern crossing the sky. Turning his head, he could see the glue and bits of cut balsam that made up the buildings. He felt like he'd always seen this, only he hadn't noticed.

Nothing was real. This city was a model on a table, at the whim of an old Maker in a world of absolute nightmares.

Did the necromancers know? No, he didn't think so. Nekravé seemed to only care about the books, she knew nothing of what moved about her in the darkness.

He took the knife from the newspaper as he approached a trash can and tossed it in. To his surprise, it speared cleanly through and out the other side of the can like it was paper and stuck in the brick walkway almost to the hilt.

Staring at it, then looking around to see if anyone was watching, he snatched it up by the paint-spattered handle and gently folded the knife back into his newspaper. The Maker's knife could cut through the world.

He waited on Mr. Beraghar's lofty landing platform, holding his newspaper, looking out. He felt like he could see forever. How far did the model go? People lived out there on the edges of the city, so what did they see when they looked out?

He'd hidden weapons around the platform a week ago in anticipation of this moment, but now he didn't care. They were props in a play.

"Toten," Mr. Beraghar called, trotting down the faux front steps with his security guards in tow. "Did it go well? Did you see any ghosts?"

"It went fine," he replied in a flat voice, still staring out. Wind blew across his face from some giant fan on a nearby table.

"And the necromancer? You didn't tell my name, did you?"

"Nekravé is face down in a restaurant right now and will undoubtedly be coming after me as soon as she wakes."

"I can hide you."

"You can't." Toten turned to face the jovial, bearded man. "Tell me something, have you ever left the city?"

"There's no need to." He threw his hands wide. "Everything's here. Why?"

"I don't know anyone who's left the city. Not a single person. What if we can't?"

"What's this about?" Mr. Beraghar said, his smile fading.

"I'd like to go far away."

"Hah, travel, eh? Avoid the necromancers? Can't say as I'll join you. I've always thought of foreigners as barbaric and uncivilized."

Toten laughed sadly. "That's what I always thought too."

"The ring." Mr. Beraghar held out his hand.

Toten placed the handkerchief in his palm, barely making eye contact.

"What's this."

"It was damaged."

"Damaged?!" Mr. Beraghar clawed open the handkerchief and poured the pieces into his hand. His face slowly twisted in anger. "What happened?"

"Necromancer magic."

"You don't believe in magic!"

"Yet it's the truth."

"Your wife's debt is not canceled." He turned to his security guards. "Hang him from the railing and find me another thief. We'll get another ring."

They approached. Toten gently lifted the knife from its newspaper sheath, careful of the blade's edge. They glanced at it and smirked, but he'd already done this twice today, going back in time with the ring to do it again. Do it better.

The man on the right lunged, surprisingly quick. Toten could see the powerful pistons in his legs and arms working in unison. He sidestepped and slashed. Stuffing split along the man's midsection, cut wires spilled out, and he coughed a small waterfall of gears. Toten knew that wasn't what everyone else saw.

The second man, despite his partner's swift fall, was already stepping in to attack, swinging a metal bar. Toten blocked with the knife, and the man's expression turned to surprise as the blade passed through the bar like butter, sending most of it tumbling away. Toten continued his motion and stabbed into the little gearbox at the center of the man's chest.

Mr. Beraghar stood frozen for a moment, then turned and fled into his house. Toten followed up the steps and tugged at the massive door. It was heavy and it was locked, so he cut a new door through it with the knife and walked inside.

Toten returned home, exhausted. It was getting on toward dinner time, and Thierra was cooking. Waiting for him. She turned as he opened the door, all her whirring parts now visible to his eyes, and ran into his arms.

"You did it?" she cried, hugging him tightly.

"I did it."

"And Mr. Beraghar has forgiven the debt?"

"We talked for a while, and Mr. Beraghar was most gracious. He forgives everything but he says you're not to gamble in his halls anymore." Toten was glad that Mr. Beraghar was a coward as heart. He hadn't had to hurt him.

Thierra pulled back, looking at him. He could see her, the old her, if he didn't look too hard.

"What was the job?" she asked. "Tell me. Are we in danger from the Baron?"

He stepped around her and pulled a bottle of expensive liqueur from a high shelf. His pour was generous. She waited.

Leaning back against the counter, he smiled at her. "It has nothing to do with the Baron, but I can't tell you anything else. I probably never can."

She looked frustrated, but he was firm. He'd have to deal with Nekravé and the Necromancer's Guild eventually, but that wouldn't be much of a problem. He'd buy them off with stories of the necromantic realm.

It didn't matter. Nothing really mattered, did it? He had the clock-ring and the knife, and he could steal anything, anywhere, at any time.

He pulled her into another hug and closed his eyes against his new vision. Tears gathered. Love was what mattered.

Something scratched inside the walls.

Jeffrey Lyman is an engineer in the New York City area. His work has appeared in the anthologies *Sails and Sorcery* from Fantasist Enterprises, New Blood from Padwolf Publishing, and *Breach the Hull, So It Begins, By Other Means, Best Laid Plans,* and *Dragon's Lure* from Dark Quest Books. He was co-editor of *No Longer Dreams* and all four volumes of the award-winning *Bad-Ass Faeries* anthology series. He is a 2004 graduate of the Odyssey Writing School, and won 2nd place in the fourth quarter of the 27th Annual Writers of the Future Award.